Herman M. Moos

Mortara

Or, the pope and his inquisitors. A drama. Together with choice poems

Herman M. Moos

Mortara
Or, the pope and his inquisitors. A drama. Together with choice poems

ISBN/EAN: 9783337048969

Printed in Europe, USA, Canada, Australia, Japan

Cover: Foto ©Andreas Hilbeck / pixelio.de

More available books at **www.hansebooks.com**

MORTARA:

OR

THE POPE AND HIS INQUISITORS.

A DRAMA.

TOGETHER WITH

CHOICE POEMS.

BY H. M. MOOS.

CINCINNATI, O.,
Published by Bloch & Co., Israelite Office, 32 Sixth Street.
1860.

CHARACTERS.

MORTARA—A Hebrew merchant of Rome.

BENJAMIN—His Son.

JEPHTHAH—Nephew of Mortara.

ABRAHAM—A Hebrew school-teacher.

JUDAH—A youth in the employ of Mortara.

LEON—A Hebrew peddler.

JOSEPH—A Hebrew peddler.

NATHAN—A youth in the employ of Mortara.

POPE PIUS.

SAVELLI—A Cardinal.

BEDINI—A Bishop.

LUDOVICO, PEDROLDA. } Monks and Inquisitors.

LAWRENCE—A Friar.

MONTEFIORE—A Hebrew minister from England.

FRANCE, PRUSSIA, BAVARIA, AUSTRIA. } Ministers to Pius.

1ST. JAILOR.

2D. JAILOR.

YULAH—Wife of Mortara.

CORNELIA—A nun in love with Jephthah.

RIFKA—A sister to Leon, in employ of Yulah.

PRIORESS.

JAILORS, INQUISITORS, OFFICERS and VIRGINS.

SCENE.—Rome, in Italy.   TIME.—Nineteenth Century.

MORTARA:

Or, THE POPE AND HIS INQUISITORS.

ACT FIRST.

SCENE 1st.—A ROOM IN MORTARA'S DWELLING.

Present—*Mortara, Yulah, Judah, Leon and Nathan.*

MORTARA.—Then since 't hath pleased High Heaven,
To wave me on the steady soaring pinions of exterminating
    Time,
Thro' the labyrinthian groves of Nature's spring and summer,
Into the golden paradise of mellowed autumn:
To delight at the recollections of the dim and buried past,
When fire-forged youth sailed on the ship of sky-born Hope,
Into the safe harbor of firm and settled manhood:——
Since He vouchsafed me in His grace a noble looking boy;—
Aye, the comforting prop of hoary and declining age
To lay his silver-sprinkled head, without
The cold reception, or a harsh response
To the childish queries of promoted years:
It were, good wife,
A deep and unforgivable sin, in sooth,
To crave the pearls, now sparkling in the vista of the past,
Whiles healthful memory retails out to us,
The jewels fostered in the volume of the brain.——
But where 's my child? My Benjamin?
I have not seen the boy since day-break.——
How comfortless would be our hearth, good wife,
Without this treasure of a boy!

2

YULAH.—Thy son, dear husband, I, to Abraham, the teacher,
Have dispatched this morn. He will return not home,
Until the sun doth sink beyond the western hills.

MORTARA.—'T was wise of thee, to send him thither, wife.
For I would rather have him harnessed in
Yon teacher's simple garb of unpretending virtue,
Than see the boy equipped
In the chameleonized garb of worldly policy.
For know, good wife, a virtuous man reared up
To serviceable prime, is nature's noblest work,
As well as doting parents' proudest boast.

YULAH.—I 'm glad, kind husband, that this duty done,
Has met approval in thy judgment's eye.——
A son so nobly fathered and so wisely schooled,——
As yon teacher's wise as virtuous, will be
An ivy-mantled oak to us and Israel.

MORTARA.—Well said, indeed, my true and loving wife.
Our boy shall be a justice-loving man.
Though like the storm-tossed bark upon the sea,
That 's dashed from howling wave to howling wave,
Until some huge and angry billow hurls,
To rack, this at its mercy-seeming sail
High as the starry vault; but foiled, finds her
Still coursing on the ocean's frowning brow,
Toward the magnet-counselled roads:
So shall our boy be nearer God's protection,
The more fanatic sects would mischief study
Against High Heaven's obedient servant,
Whiles he shall firmly steer his soul, untainted
By their keen conceits, into the paradisian valley
Of immortality ——But these are vain
And idle words. The vile inquisitors
Are buried in the blood-filled ocean of
Their butcheries. Religious liberty
Is granted almost o'er civilization.——

So let us entertain no fears; the fool
Does borrow cancerous troubles
Which being harbored stops the fount of joy.

YULAH.—I hope his life
Will be a useful and a happy one.

MORTARA.—Amen to thy wish. It weaves bright garlands
'round
Th' enchanted lamp of onward beckoning hope.

YULAH.—He is a mild and harmless boy.

MORTARA.—Just like thyself,
A wandering angel from a brighter sphere,
His face, like thine, is but the blushing sky.
Where only, tears in pity shed, can chase away
The sportive smile. To look upon his infant brow,
Does fill my heart with joy. For there methinks,
His winning glance reflects again, and yet again
Thy soul-engaging countenance. So I
Beheld it, dearest Yulah, when youth and passion
Fired our blood into a virtuous love.

YULAH.—I yet remember well the day,—aye, the very hour,
When I one summer eve heard in yon vale
Of fragrant flowers, those holy, tender vows
The thought of which yet thrills my soul with ecstacy.

MORTARA.—That day is chronicled in my brain, good Yulah,
When thou reluctantly becamest my wife,
And brought'st sweet comfort in the poor man's house.
But now, thank Heaven, no longer poor. For look!
My caskets and my trunks are filled with gold,
Which I by labors of the speculative mind
Have honestly acquired,——A will I 'll make.
'T is meet that I should write a testament,
And banish from the mind all cares and troubles
Not befitting well my years. Death's minister,
Grey-bearded age courts but a short—short season;

Then points toward the grave and mother earth.——
Judah!

JUDAH.—Dear Sir!

MORTARA.—Step this way, Judah! I would speak to thee.

JUDAH.—I 'm here and at your service.

MORTARA.—Soon wilt thou serve me hence, where I no longer
Shall thy service crave. But few short hours are mine,
And then the lease I have on life is out.——
Thou shouldst have had reward even ere this time,
But wealth, mine ever faithful friend,—aye wealth
In youthful hands oft proves more dangerous,
Than poison which destroys the carnal man.

JUDAH.—I never wanted aught, that you thought proper to
withhold.

MORTARA.—But now since manhood crowns thy furrowed
brow,
And reason quelled rebellious passion,
Which undecided youth not knows to subjugate:
I may entrust thee with that wealth, which I
Long since allotted for thy special use.

JUDAH.—I know not how to thank you.

MORTARA.—By promising to make good use thereof.

JUDAH.—You have taught me how to spend it wisely.

MORTARA.—So thou (to Nathan) shalt in my will remember-
ed be;
And thee, (to Leon) for thy kind sister's sake, as well
As for thine industry I 'll not forget.

NATH. and LEON.—A thousand thanks.

MORTARA.—O! rather thank Jehovah, who has made
Me but the happy instrument to give!——
But see! where now my nephew does appear!——
How noble and erect his firm-joined limbs
The lithe and well-shaped body swing.

Enter JEPHTHAH.

Welcome, nephew, we have missed thee here indeed.

JEPH.—I hope to be excused for this delay,
Since business of importance called me hence;
Which hardly was dispatched,—now uncle it was so,—
At once I homeward did direct my steps.

MORTARA.—"Now, uncle it was so,"—that 's very good.
Not stopped to catch bright glimpses of her eyes?—
Aye, youth; I 'll guess thy secret happiness:
Thou think'st thyself in love.—Look, how he blushes!

JEPHTHAH.—Tush, tush!—If but to think thyself in love
Is attended with such bliss, to love indeed
Would be beyond endurance and description.
Although I must confess the pleasing fault,—
Since you will have it one,—of loving her
Who 's pure as well as fair, kind uncle.

MORTARA.—The fault, good youth, is not in loving,—no;
But in the object of thy tender love.
Hast brought it to her knowledge?—What! not yet?
I mean the purport of this admiration;
Dost dally with her heart? fie, fie! 't were shame.

JEPHTHAH.—No, no, kind uncle; orphans never trifle
With pure affections, smiling cherubim
Distilled into a true and spotless soul.——
Although I have not ventured yet to chime
My heart's desire to mild Cornelia,
Who in her downy robe of innocence
Resembles more some straying Peri of
Lost paradise than frail and mortal dust,
That 's animated but to live a weathercock.

MORTARA.—And why, I pray thee, kept'st thy thoughts from
her?

JEPHTHAH.—She is not one of Israel's daughters.
2*

MORTARA.—It makes no odds if she be virtuous.———
And knows she not a Hebrew courts her love?

JEPHTHAH.—She ne'er inquired of me what I profess.

MORTARA.—'T is strange, though trusting as fond lovers are,
Forget they should a point, where love itself
Too often wrecks; and hopes as bright as summer-morns
Too often die in disappointment's breath.———
Such whirlpools of contention holy sects create.———
Come, nephew, answer these few questions here
Which I deem necessary to put on thee,
As it behooves a Hebrew and a man.

JEPHTHAH.—I never have
In words or deeds my kindest friend deceived.

MORTARA.—I doubt not, good Jephthah,
The honesty of thy intents.   But since
It is a privilege of old and reason-balanced age,
To reach counsel to the sapling, and hail back
With sound advice the straying judgment of
Youth's wavering mind, I hold it now my duty
To tell thee thou understand'st not well
The grand position thou hast just assumed
In connection with this Christian damsel.———
Thou wouldst marry her?   Wouldst not?

JEPHTHAH.—My heart's desire points to this blissful consummation.

MORTARA.—If by that consummation, youth, the bliss
That should attend the after years be not consumed,
'T were then indeed a blissful consummation.

JEPHTHAH.—She seems as gentle and as pure a maid,
As ever crowned a yearning lover's hopes.

MORTARA.—So looked the Gazanian harlot,
Ere she undid the lion-muscled Samson.

JEPHTHAH.—The double-faced Delilah enticed her lord,
But to receive a certain sum of silver.

MORTARA.—But should this pure and virtuous-seeming maid,
The too much trusting Jephthah lure into
The web which hideth her deformities !
Perhaps to satisfy the ticklish flesh ?————
I say, "perhaps"—her blood be prodigal;——
Aye, aye, to satisfy the ticklish flesh,
The which no sooner is acquired, than tired,
But sure of thee, she 'd show the frailties
Which under a fair mask did sleep the while.

JEPHTHAH.—She never breathed one word to prove her aught
Than what I vouched: a virtuous and a gentle dame.

MORTARA.—The marriage-seeking maid does hide her faults,
And for a while subdues her evil passions.
Will study silver-ringing laughter,—golden smiles,
To bait the unsuspecting youth withal.
But when the holy rites of Hymen bound
The lovers in the ties death only severs :
Then she 'll throw off occasion-suiting smiles,
And look the frail and infirm thing she is.——
Take heed ! take heed !

JEPHTHAH.—'T were wiser far,
To let these strife-breeding elements
Ne'er more escape the chain discretion forged,
Until the gentle usage of her lord,
Dissolves the uncouth passions of the wife,
To sighs of smiling trust and tears of fond attachment.

MORTARA.—It will indeed a blessing be, when wives
As much take care to keep the husband's love in thrall,
As to win them to the marriage altar.————
But I have somewhat strayed,
From what I fain would speak and see thee do.
I 'd have thee prove the maiden thou so lovest,
Worthy of Mortara's nephew; and if

She stands the trial well—thou canst marry her.
But ere thou makest her wife,
Teach her the laws of Moses and of Israel;
So that thy children grow not up apostates
To thy faith, by what the mother may instil.

JEPHTHAH.—I am resolved to question her upon this theme.

MORTARA.—Then speed thee to her bower.
And if she be an angel like my Yulah
Confess thy love and laugh at bachelors.——
Come, let us go the evening air to woo
And watch the Day-God tinge the western view.
(*Exit* MORTARA leaning on JUDAH & LEON; YULAH & NATHAN.)

JEPHTHAH.—Now hie me thence, O, heavenly power!
No longer will I dally with thy love,
Since I permission have to wed thee to my bed!
I straightway go to try mine art in love,
Then carry to my home the Fairy of my dreams.
Exit JEPHTHAH.

———

SCENE 2d.—NEAR A CLOISTER.
Enter POPE PIUS, LUDOVICO AND LAWRENCE.

PIUS.—Will the bishop come?

LUDOVICO.—He will attend your Holiness
Whene'er you think it meet to give him audience.

PIUS.—Tell him to meet us after mass.——And thou,
Good friar Lawrence, get thee to the cardinal.
Acquaint him of our wish to see him at the chapel.

LAWRENCE.—We will straightway on our mission forth.
PIUS.—The holy virgin will protect you.——

(*Exit* LUDOVICO and LAWRENCE.)
Now from yon cloister swells a solemn peal,
Shrieking through the air like to the knell of death;
And all the credulous who hear this sound
The summons answer at the Catechumen.

Now priest and monk around the hallowed shrine,
Confessions hear—from sins the lives absolve;
Presuming thus upon their natural gifts,
By claiming power beyond their reach and bent,
To gull withal the trusty and the shallow-brained.——
But now our church which stood as firm as rock,
And mightier than the gale that sweeps the sea
From the fathomless deep to burst the gates of heaven,
Seems tottering from her blood-bought dignity,
To which our holy predecessors reared her.——
And shall we—we, the Papal See of Rome,
Look tamely, mutely on her waning strength,
Nor seek an antidote to cure the cancer,
Which yearning after freedom has imbibed?——
Since Wisdom's torch a bright effulgence throws,
O'er all who ope their eyes to catch the light,
That once alone by priests and monks enjoyed
Gave strength and power to our holy church;—
Since common rabble do inhale the air
Progressive knowledge wafts into their homes
Where ignorance and superstition held their court:
It fears us much to keep that structure safe,
Which smooth deception from the flame of truth concealed.
No longer will we dally with our foes!——
Our wits must be at work conceiving means
To stop the pending danger ere it be too late.——
We dare not show our fears, nor seem the least concerned!
Else lose the power the bloody crusades gained,
And Pontiffs shielded with a brandished steel.——
What! by St. Peter! there was once a time
When frowns but seen upon our Papal brow,
Struck all the world with terror and dismay.——
Kings,—aye, crowned heads.have in terrific awe
Bent low their knee, and willingly became
The servants of our holy church; and thus
Were nothing more than echo is to sound.——

14

Shall Pius like a cuckold from his purpose flinch?
And not reclaim the power, with which our church
Invested him?———By the sainted virgin!
It shall be reclaimed! and that by Pius.———
We 'll deal the blow where least resistance greets our arms;
Until we 've gathered strength by what 's destroyed;
Then shall our work a bolder aspect wear,
And every creed that differs with our faith,
Shall in the inquisition be convinced,
That Rome is strong;—our downfal but a myth.—
Some few weeks hence, a daring, Hebrew youth,
Thus loudly thought as we did pass him by;
Let us think:———

"The freedom England gave to Jews,
We 'll force from Rome, should she refuse."

Wait, wretch! Cornelia's comeliness will soon
Attract thee to thy ruin—in spite of all thy threats.
And then—look out! look out, envenomed viper!
We 'll cool that blood rebellious in thy veins,
Ere thou canst poison breathe into the mind.———
The torch and rack we 'll once more bring in use;
The Protestant must weep when we have done with Jews.

Exit PIUS.

SCENE 3d.—THE CONVENT-GARDEN.
Enter CORNELIA.

CORNELIA.—He is not here.—O, may
He never come again! though by that wish
I banish hence the solace of my life.
Holy mother! O, have mercy on my weakness!—
Judge not too harshly: for I am—no, no—
I know no longer what I am, since vows
Now violated mar the sky of chastity.———
And yet I do but execute his laws;
The dreaded mandates of his holiness,
To wander from yon gloomy convent walls,

Where sisters
Consecrated to monasterial service,
Apart from all the joys of earth, must mope
In melancholy seclusion.——I have ensnared
The Hebrew youth, as it hath been desired,
To clear our church of this bold heretic.——
They 'd have me call for help at his approach.
That monks and priests lodged in some thicket near
Could take him in arrest for luring off,
A virgin from this unadulterated state.
But he, O holy saint!
Whom it is my duty to betray—destroy,
Inspired me with his manly daring;
And roused within the smothered flame of love
Into an agitated blaze, which like
A stream of lava courses through my veins.——
I have deceived with falsehoods and inventions,
The servants of his holiness, who lay
In wait for Jephthah. I told them he would not
Meet me again, until another month
Rolled o'er the track of time.—But ah! they ne'er
Shall take my lover while I live.—No never!——
O, what bliss to hear his deep, sonorous voice,
That lulled to sleep Cornelia's sacred vows;
To see his eyes more fiery than the sun
Rest on my features when they languished straight.——
If 't is a sin to love yon Hebrew youth
Whose heart is beating with a soul divine,
More bliss would be in violating Thy dread laws,
Than could be banished from the feasty mind
By all the stings and miseries, with which
Grieved conscience could upbraid and wound the soul.
I will tell him to leave this place at once;
To shun Cornelia and the nunnery;——
What! become a traitress to our holy church?
Abuse the confidence she placed in me?

Disclose her secrets to her bitter foe ? —
Never, never !—And yet I fain would save the youth.
I can not sacrifice my faith——nor him ;
So let me bleed for both, I truly love.——
I will abuse—insult him in contempt ;
With speech of insolence I sneer him off.
He will despise me from that moment on ;
Forget this nun ; avoid the dangerous snare.
Thus free I whom the pontiffs would destroy,
Whiles for my disobedience to the shrine
I 'll lead a life of penitential sorrow.
But here he comes—

Enter JEPHTHAH.

What wants the Hebrew here ? he is too bold
To risk his life upon forbidden ground.

JEPHTHAH.—Those treasures are most prized, which we
  through danger gain.
But why art thou so sad—so shy to-day ?
Speak, bright angel ; let me know the cause.

CORNELIA.—Wouldst know why I am distant to the world ?
Why shrink to gaze upon thy countenance ?
Give me thine ear, and draw the sentence in :
I am a sister, sworn to endless purity,
Who would deserve the holy virgin's blessing
By strict obedience to the laws prescribed.
Then Hebrew go ; ask me no questions more ;
Depart, and leave Cornelia for herself.

JEPHTHAH.—Ah, me ; how little have I dreamed of this,
That thou, my guiding star, wouldst bid me leave,
What this poor orphan only loves on earth.

CORNELIA.—The cloister is my home ;——
The smiling world in all her beauty 's thine.

JEPHTHAH.—Sweet nun, unsay what thou hast uttered here ;
My love and life breathe in thy destiny.

CORNELIA.—Behold me, Hebrew; see this infirm maid,
Forgetting thus the duty to her saint.
Has she not left her shrine against her vow,
Once more to look on earth—on thee ?

JEPHTHAH.—O, were I certain that my boldness, love,
Made thee forget Jehovah in thyself,
I would reproach myself and weep for thee.
Being convinced, that woman was not born,
To live in isolation from the world:
But be consoling partner of the sterner sex,
And jointress to man's short and happy state:—
I, strengthened by the weight of this mine argument,
Have urged this suit of love to thee, which, I
Was vain enough to think, would not rejected be.

CORNELIA.—Couldst thou convince Cornelia's struggling soul,
But of the truth of this assertion made:
By loving thee, fair stranger, as I do
I'd violate no law divine,—my soul
Would dance; my heart would leap with joy.

JEPHTHAH.—There is no law in holy scripture found,
That does demand of us our wretchedness.

CORNELIA.—'Ah, but the canon law prohibits those,
Who serve the holy virgin at the shrine,
To seek the pleasures of an active life.

JEPHTHAH.—This Roman rule stands null and void, sweet nun,
Since hostile to the laws of Nature; which
By Jehovah were established. ·

CORNELIA.—The monasterial law forbids carnal knowledge.

JEPHTHAH.—The physical law demandeth it, which is
An ordinance of Heaven. And all the rules
Conflicting in the least with Nature's wants
Prove pregnant with calamities.

CORNELIA.—In m'sery of life our fortitude is tested.
3

JEPHTHAH.—But by adhering to the laws of God,
We do protect the functions of the flesh and mind,.
And thereby gain true happiness.

CORNELIA.—Perfect happiness is unattainable·
In the murky regions of mortality.

JEPHTHAH.—In striving to obtain exalted bliss,.
We feel more joy than by possessing it.

CORNELIA.—The sweet assurance of deserving it,
Does make us live in hope.

JEPHTHAH.—They do not merit bliss, who are the cause .
Of their own wretchedness.

CORNELIA.—Yet those are never in distress—nor woe,
Who do believe in holy Mary's faith.

JEPHTHAH.—They serve not God, who by "BELIEVING" think
Their every mission is completed..

CORNELIA.—By believing in His laws, we Reverence
To His wisdom show.

JEPHTHAH.—But only by enforcing them, we prove
Their usefulness.

CORNELIA.—The believing do enforce.

JEPHTHAH.—The secluded can't enact.

CORNELIA.—Th' enactor should well know his part.

JEPHTHAH.—The heart must fill the station of a prompter.

CORNELIA.—Mine has incited me to love bold Jephthah.

JEPHTHAH.—And mine now whispers that I gained my point·

CORNELIA.—A sacred vow still claims me at the shrine.

JEPHTHAH.—It is a lesser wrong to solve the vow
Which teems with woes, than to observe it.

CORNELIA.—I will no longer with thee cope, since with.
Sophistic eloquence thou wouldst convert
Me even from conviction.

JEPHTHAH.—O, let thy heart subdue
The opposition of the mind to truth.

CORNELIA.—Were I to listen to my heart's appeal,
I 'd doom my soul to endless misery.

JEHTPHAH.—Let me but call thee mine,
And aged Mortara will convince thee of thy wrong.

CORNELIA.—Mortara? Did I hear thee say—Mortara?
He is a Hebrew and a heretic.
A heavy curse now rests upon his head.

JEPHTHAH.—I am his brother's son, and do profess
The same religion he so glories in.

CORNELIA.—Oh! may the virgin show her pity to thy soul.

JEPHTHAH.—I fear not consequences after death,
Since I respect my Maker and His laws.

CORNELIA.—I shrink in horror at the terrible thought,
That calls to mind the sufferings of thy soul,
For having spurned the virgin and her son.

JEPHTHAH.—No, no, sweet dove; let thy cerulean eyes
Assent to be the Hebrew's sun through life;
And in their melting lustre let him thrive,
And think it paradisian luxury.

CORNELIA.—I am resolved to spend the days of life,
Far from my friends, in virginal obscurity.
There will I crave sweet pardon for past sins;
For my disgrace and crime to dally with a Jew.

JEPHTHAH.—O, may this prove to be the only sin
For which thou need'st forgiveness from High Heaven,
And all the angels will bow down at once,
In recognition of thine innocence.

CORNELIA.—Thy tongue is ever ready to defend
The reputation of thy trifling race.

JEHTHAH.—I 'm one of Israel's most unworthy sons,
Whose characters are far beyond reproach.

CORNELIA.—Their stubbornness and ignorance withal,
Made them objects of derision and contempt.

JEPHTHAH.—O, girl! these words of thine unbridled speech,
Far more distressed this weeping soul, than hadst
Thou lodged a poisoned arrow in my heart.
I well perceive the knowledge of our traits
Is limited with thee; else wouldst not thus
Accost the heir of Israel's pride and worth.
The Hebrews are no object of derision,—
At least not to the just and candid mind;—
They are a virtuous, crime-suppressing race.
But being champions of religious liberty;
Encouragers of arts and sciences,
They thereby proved the Roman clergy's bitterest foes,
Who only by enthralling mind and soul,
Can wield their scepter safely. The Hebrew's
Noble deeds they'd bury in the welkin
Of obscurity; while the disapproved acts
Of a single miscreant, are heralded
From pole to pole as the effects of Judaism.
This is the reason, convent sister, that
The credulous believe us pitiful.
Nay, nay; start not at this unpolished speech;
I will not breathe offensive words to thee,
If even Jephthah's heart be wounded to the core.

CORNELIA.—Should I have wrongly judged, I hope thou wilt
forgive.

JEPHTHAH.—Forgive thee, Cornelia?
Aye, hadst thou slain this orphan-youth, even then
He would thy pardon crave before the all-wise Judge.
In spite of what occurred I prize thee still.
Then hear me vow no maid to love but thee,
Whom now I leave forever with a prayer:
That God may be thy Guardian through this life.
Once more let me behold those gentle eyes,

For now the future greets me with black clouds.
Cornelia, if I ever breathed a word,
Which may have fallen harshly on thine ears,
I from my heart repent.—I 'll leave thee now,
As thou didst bid me go.   God bless thee e'er;
It is the orphan's wish.

Exit JEPHTHAH.

CORNELIA.—He's gone!
With him departs my bliss and happiness.
'T was hard to wound his tender heart;—it was.
But I have saved him from the Pontiff's wrath,
And in that thought I 'll comfort take.
Now penitent I seek once more the shrine;
The sin of loving him is Nature's—but not mine.

Exit CORNELIA.

SCENE 4th.—INSIDE OF A CHAPEL.
Enter POPE PIUS, SAVELLI, BEDINI.

PIUS.—If this digested scheme
Intrusted to our English faction, had
But taken its desired effect on Britain's Peers
Who have in favor of admitting Jews
To parliament decided:—then we could 've braved
The opposition fearless of consequences.

BEDINI.—The clergy has once more
Revolting Europe to our yoke subjected.

SAVELLI.—Besides, I firmly do believe, your Grace
That yet we 'll fetter Protestant England,
And then her freedom-spreading pinions crop so short,
That they will need no second plucking.

PIUS.—I tell thee, Cardinal: England slipped our grasp;
Nor all the wily intrigues, concocted in
The subtle brain, her independence now
Can fetter in the Roman chain.   For mighty foes,
Inflexible as Lebanonian Cedars,

3*

Have lately gained possession of the Council-bench :
Dictating laws such as to *air* dissolves,
Our bright anticipation of universal power.

BEDINI.—We, their progressive strides can yet restrain,
As easily————

PIUS.—As stay
Infuriated tigers or starving wolves,
From leaping on the frightened lamb.—Can yet
Thy calculating eye sum up a wholesome hope,
Though some experience chiseled on thy mind :
"The Hebrew rises in the Pontiff's fall ?"
And now the vipers have achieved their purpose ;
And in the radiance of their dawning sun
Our blended star appears a dying flame.

SAVELLI.—But, holy Pontiff, deign to hear my words :
There 's nothing bad but what could be far worse.
We can effect a jarring strife at least
By sowing discord where the Jew presides,
Ascribing it to their dissentious ways.
This imputation shall our Upas-tongue
Breathe into the infectuous air ; and those
Inhaling then this deleterious atmosphere,
Will foul suspicion harbor in their brain.
This done, such ripened opportunity
Our watchful faction not neglects ; but will
With hints of treachery the press besprinkle.
It creates doubts about their loyalty,
And thereby cause mistrust in parliament.

PIUS.—Ah ! thy measured words
Infused once more consoling strength, Savelli !
And sceptered Pius feels again his Majesty.
By St. Peter ! we will not deduct one jot
From our resolve : but will our rites enforce,
With such a rigor and asperity,
That neither mitigation nor abatement,

Shall from our Papal crown be looked for.
Good Bishop! what says Cornelia, the nun?
Has her shrouded wile and her magnetic beauty
Failed to attract the busy viper's attention?

BEDINI.—She has been sounded well upon this theme,
By Ludovico, the inquisitor.
He has reported to me yester-morn,
The sister's words, which by your holy leave
I 'll simply here repeat.

PIUS.—Let us hear them, Bishop.

BEDINI.—So runs the narrative: The Hebrew youth, —
I speak of Jephthah, the threatening mad-cap, —
Has only with her once conversed, and this
At such a time, when neither monk nor priest
Was in the reach of voice; and therefore could
Not execute your dread command, as promptly
As her duty did desire.   And then beyond
Her expectation, she but found this youth
At first so cold to all her fond entreaties
That it took all her wit to make him yield.
He promised her a visit in a month,
Where first Cornelia intercepted him.

CARDINAL.—It is indeed a narrative.

PIUS.—We much mistrust this duteous nun, good friends,
Since this creation wears too much the spotless face
Of truth methinks; she finds him first too cold
To the entreaties of impassioned youth; —
And then it took her wit to make him yield; —
Wit was successful where lewd beauty failed?
Tut! tut! Cornelia is deceiving us.
This begotten matter is too smooth,
All marrow and no bones; besides we 've heard
That she of late grew much to musing,
A doubtless proof of something rotten.
We 'll question her ourself; for we much fear
His shape made love predominant in her.

Enter OFFICER.

OFFICER.—The fathers, Ludovico and Pedrolda .
Crave admittance to your Holiness.

PIUS.—Let them enter.

Exit OFFICER.

By St. Paul! we must subdue revolting brains,
Such as this Jephthah's prove to be. For his
Rebellious thoughts may breed a nest of traitors.
Thus with this single blow we 'll terrify
The world and silence sharp-edged treason.
Be it hid on Persian plains, where fierce hyenas
Howl their wrath around the rifled grave;
Or on Gran-Sasso's star-stabbing peaks
Where vultures brood o'er their rapacious aims.

Enter LUDOVICO and PEDROLDA.

But what have you, good fathers, to impart?

LUDOVICO.—Since 't is the the pleasure of your Majesty
To know the purport of our presence here:
We 'd beg your gracious leave to tax your ear
Until we have related to your Grace
A servant's strange confession, in which
The church would by your wisdom be advised.

PIUS.—What black transgression pricks the conscientious
knave,
That absolution was denied?

LUDOVICO.—Her trespass, Holy Sire, is not in losing faith,
But by enforcing it: and therefore was
Of her black sins absolved. But, Sire, the thing
That puzzles now our celibatic set,
Is how to act, with what she has confessed.
Most holy Pontiff hear:—A Hebrew child,
The servant mentioned, baptized some years since,
In the name of Father, Son and Holy Ghost.
The child has grown to be a sprightly boy,
Whom yet his father weans to Jewish faith.

PIUS.—Whose nimble loins wantoned for this progeny?

LUDOVICO.—He into being sprung,
By Mortara's lascivious desires.

PIUS.—Mortara didst thou say? By St. Paul! we have
But prayed for chance, and now it stares us in the face!
What we by wile and stratagem would gain,
Will justice seem in us to claim. Why, 't was he,
Who in his grief o'er Jephthah's early death,
Should be the first to feel our march to power,
Was now by stern browed fortune singled out
To be our maiden-victim, as we planned.
His child we 'll steal, and Jephthah will we slay,
Then let the hoary wretch complain of us.
Hence! and in the holy inquisition's name
Claim this boy; but if they should refuse
To give him up at your request:—then snatch
Him from the mother's breast or father's arms.
No matter how you gain possession of the brat.
We do command you bring him hither straight.

LUDOVICO.—It will be midnight ere we 'll reach the place.

PIUS.—It is the very time for Rome's inquisitors
To seek their sleeping victims.—What! still here?
Are we no longer Pontiff of our church,
That low-born minions dare to disobey
Our dread commands?—Inquisitors, speed quickly on!
Or by St. Paul! ye 'll suffer under the ban.

LUDOVICO.—O, holy Sire, too much we do respect
Your high commands that we should waver in
The service now required.—We crave forgiveness.—
It was the time, as we at such late hours
Have never yet been sent till now, that made
Us think, you were but ill acquainted, as .
To where Mortara lives.—Your pardon, Sire.—

PIUS.—'T is granted.
            (*Exit* LUDOVICO AND PEDROLDA.)

To night, most holy friends, the close-barred gates,
Which too long have on rusty hinges hung,
Shall creaking welcome this Mortara's son.
Stop;——he shall be treated with a better fare,
Since 't is advisable to use him well,
So he may find delight in sacramental rites.
We 'll consecrate him to our holy church;
We need more priests; more monks—our faction 's small..—
But let this rest till morn, and now to mass.—
Hark! the convent-bell peals forth the hour of seven;
Then let 's go in,—but first put on a face of heaven.

      Exit POPE PIUS, LUDOVICO and PEDROLDA.

    SCENE 5th.—A ROOM IN MORTARA'S DWELLING.
        Enter JEPHTHAH.

  JEPHTHAH.—Despised me,—rejected me,—and thought it
Condescension to treat me with civility,—
To notice me.—Thus much her words expressed.
To think her wise, aye, virtuous and pure,
Would argue me devoid of all those three.—
Now let me analyze the subject some.
If she be wise and guided by discretion,
Why suffered she the first intrusion made?
Wherefore to wait until I wooed her love,
To bid me go and leave the nunnery,
When she was dedicated to the shrine
And could have stopped advances she approved?
For by Jehovah! she seemed pleased at first,
And was right happy in my company;—
I know she was—I saw it in her eyes;
They sparkled tenderly at my approach.
What right had she to listen to my vows?—
She was then a nun as well as she is now.—
If others can—I will not think her wise.
If she be pure and virtuous withal,
Why did she wander from the monastery,

As if designed, but to encounter me?
She could have well avoided me, instead
Of lewdly blinking and obstruct my way.
And yet, I know not why, I think her pure,
And love her as I never loved before.
Her heart is good, but, oh! her teaching's bad.
Jesuits! Jesuits! tremble in your masks,
A bitter retribution gathers o'er your heads.

(JEPHTHAH *Exit.*)

Enter MORTARA and ABRAHAM.

MORTARA.—I do entreat thee stay with us to-night,
And make us debtors to thyself once more,
For granted joys in entertaining thee.

ABRAHAM.—I would with joy accept thine offer, friend,
Were I inclined to add on what I owe,
The favors lavished by thyself on mine,
In such offenseless way and manner too,
Would even bankrupt kings of great estates,
To pay the interest of thy bounteous hands.

MORTARA.—Speak not of this as praise in me, which is
Proclaimed but simple duty in mankind.
The donor feels much happier far in dealing bliss
And comfort to the needy, than if he
Enjoyed his favored friends' munificence
To its unlimited extent.——I will
Be host o'er all frugal wants, and help
Thee while away few hours in honest cheer:
Didst hear this crash? (thunders) the air-tossed elements
Are angry now. The thick black clouds forth marshal
Noiseless to the howling battle-field. Hark! (thunder and
    lightning.)
The fire-spouting phalanxes have met at last,
And all their strength now falls in tears to earth.
Thou must partake of hospitality,
Or else offend thy friend, with thy refusal.
Here comes my wife as well as Benjamin.

The wailing voices of those dying warriors
Have in loud thunders roused the weary clay
From balmly slumber.

Enter YULAH *and* BENJAMIN.

Good Yulah! Abraham will house with us,
Until this too infuriated storm abates.

YULAH.—We will not let thee venture forth, good friend
In such a night as this.—Hear, how it thunders! (thunder.

BENJAMIN.—I feel assured my teacher will remain,
Since for his best my parents bade him stay.
Kind father, knowest thou I feel so highly pleased
When you and Abraham converse together?

MORTARA.—Why so, my Benjamin?

BENJAMIN.—Because you keep a quarrel up, in such
A pleasant manner.

MORTARA.—Thinkest so my boy?—O, Abraham, I know not
    how
To thank High Heaven for this treasure of a boy.
My hoary age would be a burthen to
These marrowless bones, could I not dream
Me back once more to flowery spring, in thus
Beholding him.—Aye, he is my very soul.
I would much rather part with life itself,
Than see the child in grief. I love him tenderly.
Look! his mother's beauty blooms afresh
On his unforrowed brow.—A kiss my boy.   (Kisses him.)

YULAH.—Thou 'lt spoil our boy with too much doting.

ABRAHAM.—No, no; Mortara raises Benjamin
To well deserve his parents' warm affections.

MORTARA.—Rear him to deserve our love?—aye, to deserve
The love of all the world besides.   We 'll have
Him schooled in the laws of great Jehovah.
His justice and his virtue shall become
An ornament on him—an honor to his mother.

BENJAMIN.—Father; kind Abraham
Has taught me how to be and live a Jew.

MORTARA.—How wouldst thou then proclaim thy faith?

BENJAMIN.—In few, short words 't is said, my father dear,
Though full of meanings great.

MORTARA.—I fain would hear them from thy ruby lips.
What is the maxim of the Hebrew race?
Impart it to me, boy.

BENJAMIN.—Respect Jehovah and thyself.

MORTARA.—Respect Jehovah and thyself.   In what
Must we disclose this reverence, grave philosopher?

BENJAMIN.—In adhering to the mandates of our Lord,
We show regard to Him, whose wisdom planned them for
The welfare of mankind; and then to follow
What our conscience us dictates, we but esteem ourselves
In doing naught save what commands respect.

MORTARA.—Why boy! this godly speech would honor throw
On graver heads than thine.—Much thanks to thee,
Good Abraham, for thus instructing him,
Mine heir, in what behooves a man to know. •
Art sleepy, boy?—put him to bed once more.—
The heavenly cannons stopped to roar, and yet
The upper ocean seems to empty all
Her watery caverns upon the earth.
Hark! heardst thou not a knock below?

ABRAHAM.—'T is but the wind that tosses to and fro.

MORTARA.—Again I hear it knock! what can this mean?
I wonder much to hear a strange appeal
At such late hour.—Is Jephthah forth, good wife?

YULAH.—I saw him enter his apartment,
As I did pass him by, to join you here.
Hark! it knocks again and louder than before.

MORTARA.—I 'll go and see—perhaps it is a homeless man.
I 'll go and see, good wife.   (*Exit.*)
4

YULAH.—What hour ? it must be dawning time of day.

ABRAHAM.—Nay, nay; we yet are in the heart of night.

YULAH.—There 's danger pending over some of us.
My soul is much oppressed with doubts and fears.
What stays him at the mansion-gate so long?

ABRAHAM.—Thou canst assert no reason why to doubt;
Therefore disperse this folly from thy mind.

YULAH.—'T is true, I have no cause for this anxiety,
And yet I can not scatter, though I would,
The harbored thoughts of fear.

ABRAHAM.—Why look! he now approaches with some guests.

MORTARA, (outside.)—Gentlemen, you do but trifle with my
    feelings,
        (*Enter* MORTARA, LUDOVICO and PEDROLDA.)
To choose this hour to frighten this old man.

LUDOVICO.—We came to claim thine offspring, in the name
Of Rome's right holy inquisition.

MORTARA.—Why, friend, for so I fain must think you;
Else you would not venture such liberties with me,
Who now emerges from the autumn of his life,
Into frosty winter's grave.—I know you do but jest.

PEDROLDA.—We are inquisitors of Rome, and now
Commanded by his Majesty, the Pope,
To seize thy christened son, or else not leave
Thy house with breath.—So speaks his holy Grace
Through his two consecrated servants.

MORTARA.—I am a Hebrew merchant;—honest—loyal.
Have labored all my life, and now I 'm old;
My wife, pray look, has seen her summer days;
This boy is all the comfort left to us.
Oh! rob us not of him,—my Benjamin;
He has been raised an Israelite in faith.

ABRAHAM.—I 'm terror-struck with these proceedings.

You can 't expect to take this boy along,
Since there 's no law, thank God, depriving man
Of his legitimate as well as only child.

LUDOVICO.—The lad was baptized while an infant sick,
And therefore is he claimed to serve His Grace.—
But we can 't dally with thee, heretic;
Give up the boy, else we 'll apply some force.

MORTARA.—Think you, that justice slumbers in eternal sleep?
Men! tread you not angry Heaven's vengeance?
Thus to defy the holiest affections of mankind—
To nullify the sacred laws of God and nature—
To trample on the dearest rights of civilized society—
To intrude into the sanctum-sanctorum of the human race—
To tear away the offspring from the sacred hearth.
Inquisitors of Rome! take hence this child of mine.
We will obey the mandates though they be unjust.
Yulah! our life has been too full of bliss,
That we should murmur at this trial sent.
Give up our child, good wife.

YULAH.—O, gentle husband, thou canst not be so cruel—
So unmerciful as to demand my—our Benjamin.
No, no; thou wilt—must refuse this foul request,
Or Yulah will alone protect her son.

MORTARA.—My heart as well as thine, good Yulah,
Now feels the torments of this cruelty.
And yet our Benjamin—our son must forth.
God wills it so.

PEDROLDA.—By our faith, we will no longer hear this prattle.
We must dispatch our duty quickly, Jew.
So hand him o'er—we 'll ask no second time.

YULAH.—I will not part with him; no!—I swear——

MORTARA.—Yulah!

Enter JEPHTHAH.

JEPHTHAH.—What noise is this that echoes dismal grief

Into the air, to mar this hallowed hour?
What! is it possible, inquisitors?

YULAH.—O, Jephthah, Jephthah do protect my son.

JEPHTHAH.—Aye, with my very life, dear aunt.

YULAH.—They would tear him from my breast.

JEPHTHAH.—They dare not.—But say again you'll take this
child,
And by High Heaven you shall repent the speech.—
Why would they wrest him from thy bosom?

MORTARA.—I pray thee, youth,
Heed not my wife's appeal—my Yulah's prayer.
O God! I suffer much to see her grief.
Inquisitors! here take my son—my more than life.
Benjamin, my boy! my blessings on thy head.
Take him.

BENJAMIN.—I will not go.—O, mother! mother!
YULAH.—My child! my child.

(YULAH faints in the arms of JEPHTHAH.)
Exit INQUISITORS and BENJAMIN.
[*End of 1st Act.*]

ACT SECOND.
SCENE 1ST.—A STREET IN ROME.
Enter JUDAH, LEON and NATHAN.

JUDAH.—Saidst thou the Pope has confiscated all
The wealth Mortara rightly owns?—That he,
Ev'n on the shallow plea of second childhood
Upon whose willow-pillared threshold
This kind, old man does seem to enter,
Would dare create himself, by virtue of
A commission from his ecclesiastical court,
Administrator o'er the sane and quick's estate?

LEON.—Sane no longer, since the Pontiff's jurisdiction
Pronounced Mortara's wits diseased and wandering.—

Be more apprised of what hath happened since
Thou left'st the dwelling of that hoary sage
To gain admittance in the nunnery.

JUDAH.—Naught evil canst communicate, that would
Surprise me now. The boldness of the Pope
Has reached its highest pitch. But as thou art
A harbinger of tidings yet more evil,
Than those already to my knowledge brought,
Impart and snap the chord of dire suspense.

LEON.—Yulah's soul sought yester-night the shadow-land;
These trials proved too much for her kind heart.

JUDAH.—What! Yulah gone?—Has she too paid the debt
We all to nature owe?—Left this world
Of care and sorrow, where hate, envy, malice,
And creeping slander send their poisonous shafts
In gratifying eagerness—at the mild
In disposition and noble in performance?—
And has her weary soul at last returned
Unto the spirits' home, where all her virtues,
Starlike 'round the throne of mercy cluster,
Within a spotless constellation of
Radiant splendor and sky-born excellence?
And her nice figure, moulded to perfection,
That bound the gazer in a trance of admiration—
Lost it its lustre and returned to common dust,
Exempt of all diseases flesh inherits here?—
She left this stage and slumbers now in peace,
Or if in yon cerulean vault awake,
Her spirit revels in the charms of its
Own purity.—Aye, she is happy whence she flew.
Let 's not in mourning pine, but go consoling
Where her absence is most deeply felt.
Let 's comfort bring to him whom fate, at once
Bereft of all those near in blood and love,
Who should his age have crowned with happiness,
Extending to the gates of far eternity.

NATHAN.—Mortara only has his warmest friends received,
And those who saw his stately form around
The ghastly Yulah kneeling, could not well
Suppress their sighs for his great misery.

LEON.—He will not listen to consoling words,
Which by discussion could allay his woes.
His bosom's froze with stoical philosophy.

NATHAN.—In his indifference to excessive joys,
Or to excruciating pain, he e'en
Does surpass th' Athenian Zeno's firm disciple.

LEON.—Nor murmurs he, so elevated are his thoughts,
At what wise Providence ordained for him.

JUDAH.—Has Jephthah been at his kind uncle's?

NATHAN.—He has been with him constantly.

JUDAH.—Know ye not where I could meet him now?

LEON.—We left him in his room,
In serious contemplations plunged.

NATHAN.—He vowed to liberate young Benjamin,
Or else to perish in the same attempt.

JUDAH.—Let us devise some plan, wherein we can
Assistance give to this bold enterprise.

LEON.—Alone will he achieve the end of his design.

JUDAH.—Were he discreet, as bold and brave, we would
Not need to fear his efforts lack success.
But whither are you bound?

NATHAN.—To seek employment in the Roman Capitol.

LEON.—And I to sell my wares, a livelihood
To earn.

JUDAH.—'T is well.   We may often meet in social bliss.
Adieu, my friends.

(*Exit* LEON and NATHAN.)

Now shall Mortara know my ill success,
That he may sue to Heaven for just redress.

Exit.

SCENE 2d.—A ROOM IN MORTARA'S DWELLING.

Present—*Mortara, Jephthah and Rifka.*

MORTARA.—Take the softest linen cloth,—aye, the softest
Thou canst find in Rome, and use it for
Her winding-sheet. Have it as white as snow,
For no less pure was Yulah. Enshroud her
Gently,—oh! gently—I prithee gently.
Let her receive in death the same mild treatment
She living e'er to all around her showed.
She was ever gentle,—ever kind.
Do not mar her form by cruel handling;
Fondle it—oh! fondle it as if it still
Possessed its priceless soul.—Rifka,
Hath she much paler grown?—more ghastly?
Or is her placid brow still colorless?

RIFKA.—It still appears of whitish hue.

MORTARA.—Hast not observed a smile, yet lingering on
Her Heaven-wrought features?—methought one slept
Upon her face, like laughing spring in the lap of morn.
Aye, unconscious of Death's thieving minister,
Who stealthily from out its sacred shrine
The spirit stole, that gave it life and reared
It to the blushing rose, which sweet content
United with confiding trust had planted on her brow.
Like as the ivy closer twines herself
Around the peerless oak, even when
The howling Storm-King felled him to the ground:—
So this one smile that did embrace her cheek
Once full with life, in death will not forsake the spot.

RIFKA.—Death marked no uncouth lines upon her brow.

MORTARA.—The hired assassin quite satisfied, when done,
With his foul deed, lacks boldness to be rifling,
Ere he parts, the slaughtered enemy. No less
Content grim-visaged death with Yulah's soul,
In his great haste to sneak away forgot to pluck

The sunny smile of innocence.—At what time
Will they inter my Yulah? Knowest thou
The hour, kind Rifka?

RIFKA.—The sunset hour was chosen by your friends.

MORTARA.—Not till then?—I 'm glad—I 'm glad.
It is the solemn time of eve when spirits
Fondly glide from heaven, again to visit earth
Reclining in the arms of parting day.
When crimson rays adorn the western firmament,
Engulfing the horizon in a golden stream
Of mellow splendor, until the misty night
Approaches in her sable gown, pronouncing thus
To nature's broad domain the death of fiery Sol.
Then, oh! then, when all the world
In gentle sleep reposes, and full around
The pale-faced moon the stars appear an angel, each
In silver-sheens enwrapped, to welcome back
The gentle dame from far intensity.
Then,—my Yulah's soul will on the perfumed breath
Of Violets sail, through realms and realms of air,
To join yon sky-abiding throng.—Now get thee
To her chamber, Rifka; and yet perform
Those little duties it requires
Her lifeless person should receive of us.

Exit RIFKA.

Last night she lay upon a bed of down;—
This night—the cold, hard clay will be her couch;
And then, who knows?—the morrow's sun may breed
A nest of busy worms to feed on flesh,
That two days past encased a soul divine.—
How strangely worketh nature on ourselves.

JEPHTHAH.—Uncle.

MORTARA.—Jephthah!—wouldst speak to me?

JEPHTHAH.—Few words, kind uncle.

MORTARA.—What is the matter with thee, youth?

JEPHTHAH.—Words, plain words, kind uncle, are too faint
    indeed,
To draw the fill of gloom now preying on my mind;
Or if even language could portray the loneliness,
Which I since childhood knew and now more deeply feel: —
What joy—what comfort could on earth make me forget,
That I without a parent, sister, brother am.
You, thank Heaven, and now our sainted Yulah,
Have shown me every kindness; aye, more than I deserved.
But oh! when I beheld the fond caresses Benjamin enjoyed,
Which parents unawares on their own offspring do bestow:
Then tears would moisten this poor orphan's eyes,
Reminding him once more that he was quite alone.
And when I knew your hopes were centered in that boy,
I sighed to think that none would e'er be proud of me,
Should once deluding fame weave laurels 'round my head.
No soothing words—no gentle and imploring eyes
To cheer me on the thorny path, which leads, 't is said,
To honor, wealth, fame and public favor.
My friendless soul did languish in the shade
Of vile neglect and lost affection's solitude;
Until indifference to what my destiny would teem,
Snapped off the spurs that pricked ambition's sides,
And made me what I am—a useless thing to all mankind.
O, uncle; I know 't is wrong to choose this solemn hour,
To speak of woes and griefs concerning me alone;
When you in your bereavement should of me receive,
The dews of consolation due to lighten your calamity.
But since misfortune has allied us closer
Than kindred blood or actions could have done,
We jointly will be satisfied in our dissatisfaction,
And thus sail hence full happy in our woes.
    MORTARA.—We must not turn lamenting from this vision
        bright,
Which only by His will a radiance 'round
Our frail existence threw; though now

Corporeally deadened to our sensual entertainment,
The mind, my boy, can penetrate the hazy clouds
Of Materiality, and soar from the narrow limits
Assigned to grosser ken into
The indefinite space of spiritual existence.
While thus we can indulge in silent conversation,
And mutely interchange our thoughts with those,
Who beckon us,
With fond entreaties from yon bliss-filled bourn,
To falter not, when galling ills by Providence ordained,
Should seek us out to test the greatness of our minds.
O, what bright thoughts! what noble, elevated feelings
Sparkle through the lustrous eyes of that individual,
Whose fortitude surpasses his misfortunes.
Then cease, my boy, to think thyself an orphan still,
When those who gave thee birth live in a happy state,
Beholding thee from yonder diamond-strand,
And all thy deeds are visible to them
The which, according to their worth or merits
Will make them smile in joy, or weep for thee.

> JEPHTHAH.—O, uncle! you have nicely shown me by this
>   picture drawn,
How parents down from Heaven gaze approvingly,
When their frail offspring spurns to meanly live
On paid applause; but wild ambition fix
On virtuous deeds and noble themes, till Providence
Records upon the scroll of endless fame,
The noble efforts misconstrued by man.
As I but live for you, pray give assent.
I have resolved to liberate your son,
To partly prove my deep-felt gratitude,
In soon restoring him to you.

> MORTARA.—Liberate my boy?—Restore him to these arms?
O, 't were joyful!—alas; it can 't be done.

> JEPHTHAH.—It shall be done, kind uncle, and this ere long.

MORTARA.—Never, never!
What! wouldst have me—me, the poor, old man,
Become chief-causer of great evils to our race?—
No, no; thou must not be so splenetive,
But keep thy temper still in reason's pale,
Since fools wage war at what High Heaven decrees.
I have dispatched the trusty Judah
To see my son, and learn the treatment he receives.

JEPHTHAH.—I hope success attends his mission.
But here he comes———

Enter JUDAH.

MORTARA.—How is he?—Didst see him—didst see my boy?
What! no?—no? not saw him?

JUDAH.—They would admit me not into his room.

MORTARA.—'T is past;—'t is over now;—he's lost forever.
This single spark of hope which I more fondly cherished,
Than the mother does her new-born infant,
Lies smothered in the heart it nourished with sweet promises.
O, could they but feel the anguish of this soul
Surcharged with woes, the which, could they cry out,
Would rend the air with dismal shrieks of pain;
Until the angry God roused by my plaints,
Would hurl more woes upon this celibatic race
Than even stubborn Pharaoh had to taste.
They are no fathers;—aye, have no children,
In whose guileless laugh, once more they hearing could behold
Young nature's fair simplicity sporting 'round their hearth.
No, no; they are no fathers.
Said I, fathers?—monsters! blood-stained knaves!
A shame to manhood!—a curse whose influence
Like winds which fan the Javanian Upas-tree
Breathe death and desolation into the atmosphere!—
O, heart! discharge not here to man thy woes;
But firmly do resolve to soar aloof
From low and base complaint, and be thyself.

JEPHTHAH.—Uncle——

MORTARA, (aside.)—Jehovah honors me withal, in testing
To the very fill my disposition with excess of grief.
Beneath that mighty weight, I'll, bending, walk erect,
And make a staff of faith, to lean thereon when tired.

JEPHTHAH.—Kindest of uncles.

MORTARA.—What wouldst have me do?

JEPHTHAH.—Do you nothing, till I have done the deed.
That will undo what others have been doing.

JUDAH.—And I, good sir, will serve you evermore.

MORTARA.—I'm poor, my son, and need thine aid no more,
For all I once possessed the Pontiff claimed.
O, Judah; he took all and left me void of means,
Save those our *Father* in his mercy granted me:
A host of friends to cheer me with their approbation
In my submission unto Jehovah's stern decrees.
I now discharge thee from my further service,
With no reward save parting blessings on thy way.—
Go, my son—go and lead an honest life—while here,
For there it will recorded blaze, till time's no more.
Thou art discharged.

JUDAH.—No, no, kind sir, I will not leave you now;
But beg you to be counting me among your trusty friends.
And thus reward your servant if you owe him aught,
By condescending from your high position,
That I may meet you with a younger brother's rights,
To share your fate in friendship's sacred bonds.

JEPHTHAH.—And I, kind uncle, will henceforth devote my
  time,
In studying how I could deserve your favors most.
Therefore be cheered, we will protect your life,
When you do prosper, only then we thrive.

MORTARA.—Friends, sons; I will accept of ye,
At least for this one night while Yulah be interred.

Come, support me;—place me by her side;
My Yulah has Jehovah now as guide.
Come, take me in.

Exit Mortara, Jephthah and Judah.

Scene 3d.—A Street in Rome.
Enter Leon and Joseph.

Leon.—A capital idea, Joseph;—a capital idea.
Thou canst thereby enrich thyself as well as me,
Nor make thy victim much poorer for this loss.
But how wilt thou his clutches so unloose,
That thou may'st safely slip the ducats from his grasp,
And fool the priest who has many a thousand gulled,
Without reminding him of what thou art about?
Ludovico is rich—yet Ludovico is a monk;
And monks, good Joe, know how to value cash,
Nor sleeps their wit to bait thee with such trash.
Such wares as these, they willingly receive,
Forgiving sinners with a mass relief.
But money, money—why money is their God,
And wouldst thou make them part from what
They fondly worship?——Get thee—get thee.
Let 's look to other quarters for some prey;
With monks I never liked to deal.

Joseph.—These monks far better to our purpose suit,
Than those who by their seeming virtue have been gulled.
Such patrons all are poor in pocket and in purse,
A testimony of a weakness in their brains.
Those who are weak and with soft folly capped
Would fear to trust us had they aught in trust.
To make a handsome speck in this our trade,
We should be courting those who think they 're wise,
And show us meek almost to low subserviency,
And stoop besides, to swell destructive vanity,
Of which they once possessed, would not expect of us
To set a trap in folly, to wisdom catch therein.
.5

Leon.—We play a hazardous game—a dangerous trick,
    friend Joe,
In daring the inventors of deceitful practices;
Whose guilt of fraud though palpable to our eyes,
So far escaped detection by some men of worth.
But even should we win—our cards be full of trumps,
We 'll lose by reputation more than we by money gain.
Although he ape-like with keen desire the stolen victuals eats,
He may like oxen, after they have taken in their food,
Again throw up the cud to ruminate, when grazing time is o'er.
He 'll soon find out that we out tricked the knave,
Then will not rest until he has us caught,
To punish us as we in truth deserve.
Yet if we could this country flee at once,
With all this wealth,—no Hebrew will respect us more.
I love to be rich—I dreamed I would be rich,
But then methought some honest hand did guide me on.
Joe, come here;—sit down by me; wilt thou, Joe?
I pray thee, friend, let 's drop this sinful conversation.
I 'm not at home in such vile deeds—in faith I 'm not.
Friend Joe, wilt know what I have always wished?
And thought of with joy?

Joseph.—Some silly speculation, I warrant.
Go on, I 'm all ears.

Leon.—So is the ass, to whom the biting whip,
Speaks louder than the angry drayman's voice.

Joseph.—And yet the stubborn ass, a safer foothold has,
Than Andalusian steeds by skilled equestrians led.
But this is not coming to the point—speak then.
I wished not to offend thee, signor Leon.

Leon.—Then make not light of what I fain would say.
Although I 'm young and reason skims the silvery waves
Of Fancy's smiling sea, deprived of steady judgment's ears.
Yet often have I in my heart revolved,
When pressed in want of food I lay me down at home,

How I in Italy could better my conditions,
To gain an easier livelihood for sister Rifka and myself.
Still like this earth which on her axis executes
A ceaseless revolution from west to east diurnally:
So this one thought its own revolvency upholds,
Since these young brains no counter-movement can create.
To solve th' enigma with a wholesome answer.
And then I 'd hunt me out some shady grove,
To woo the silence of pale solitude,
And gaze through marshaled files of trembling foliage,
Counting the myriads and myriads of glory-shining orbs,
Whose brightness seems to mock my wretched state.
At hallowed times as these I would dispel the murky gloom,
Which keeps the dame imagination in a cave of night.
To soar on blue-eyed Fancy's future gilding pinions,
From the atmosphere surrounding this our globe,
Through the world of insipid and inodorous air,
Into the holy and infinite space of liquid ether,
Where spirits in their robes of fire adorn the canopy of light.
There at last I 'd seat myself—excluded from mortality;
Viewing the numberless worlds adjusted in our system—
Their suns—their moons—their very atmospheres.
Intoxicated with the grandeur of this blazing scene,
I 'd wing myself to earth—a little twinkling speck,
To light upon the land I ever yearned to see.
Columbia!—happiest of countries!—thrice happy!
Columbia! the home of the free—th' asylum of the oppressed.
Where are no laws save such to make and keep us men.
Where no distinction between race and race is known—
Where man is judged according to his worth and not his purse.
Where freemen call thee, brother, and love thee for thy choice.
There, friend Joe, I ever prayed to have my home,
That I may unmolested exercise my rights.
    Joseph.—Why, in the deuce, dost not go there.
    Leon.—Why!—why!—canst thou ask me, why!
Thou, who see'st me from dawn of day till late at night,

With this filled basket on my hardened back,
Striving to earn my daily means, by selling ware.
To go to Columbia!—why Joseph thou art mad.
To go to Columbia!—were it to cost one penny,
I could not go as far as through the capitol.

JOSEPH.—Thou hast an excellent opportunity.
Embrace it then, thou 'lt ne'er find a second one,
Until it be too late perhaps to do thee good.

LEON.—Tempt me no further to engage in crime,
Although the bait invites me from my good intent.

JOSEPH.—Do as thou wilt—I 'll speak no more of it.
If thou art fond of poverty—humiliating poverty—
Then put this basket on thy back and sell thy ware.
No, no; I 'll say no more to thee—I swear I wont.
If thou lovest insult—degrading occupation—
Put this basket on thy back and sell thy ware.
I will not argue with thee;—to know thee spurned—

LEON.—Stop! else make me mad—thou art my counselor.
Advise me how to act the villain's part.
If play I must—I 'll play at least with art.

JOSEPH.—As luck will have it—here they come.
Ludovico and Pedrolda—two arrant knaves.
Where 's the letter I prepared?—here it is.
Now hide thyself in haste, nor do return,
Until I leave these worthies to thy skill.
Sell them thy wares; assume a frightened look,
That they suspect thee villain and a fool.
Now begone; I must be ready.
They are here. Begone.

(*Exit* LEON. JOSEPH opens the letter, but tries to hide it as
        LUDOVICO and PEDROLDA *enter.*)

PEDROLDA.—This Hebrew tries to hide a paper from our
    view;—
See, how sneakingly he moveth off.

LUDOVICO.—I 'll have the secret from yon Jew——
(He crosses JOSEPH's path and stops him from going off.)
A pleasant day, my son.

JOSEPH.—Yes, holy sirs, a very pleasant day.
(He attempts to leave but LUDOVICO intercepts him.)
LUDOVICO.—Yes, my son a pleasant day.
Were you not reading, when we came?

JOSEPH.—Nothing of importance, holy sirs.
(Tries to hurry off, but LUDOVICO stops him.)
LUDOVICO.—I'll be the judge myself; so show the manuscript.

JOSEPH.—Please, holy sir, do not insist.
It but contains some little information,
Which must not be revealed to merchants here,
As I design to make a fortune with this news.

PEDROLDA.—We 'll first investigate the paper ere he parts.
The Jews are dangerous enemies to us.

JOSEPH.—I am a stranger in the Roman Capitol.
But yestermorn I landed here from Saxony,
To trade for satins and Italian cloths.
But since you doubt mine honest word,
Read this epistle from my partner, if you will;
Informing me to purchase all the ribbons I can find;
They rose in value since I left for Rome.
Read it, good sirs, you will be secret, please.
(He hands the letter to LUDOVICO.)
A money-making speculation, I can tell you.
(LUDOVICO after reading, returns the letter.)
Have I deceived you?—no, God forbid.
Good evening;—good evening.
(*Exit* JOSEPH.)

PEDROLDA.—A well-spoken Jew, good Ludovico.
He is a business-man.—He 'll make a fortune.

LUDOVICO.—There is no doubt, he will.

PEDROLDA.—Let's get ahead of him, by buying up such ware;
5*

As we have money and can purchase at low rates.
Those Jews are greedy dogs—we 'll trade for ribbons.

LUDOVICO.—I do despise these avaricious Jews,
Who study nothing save the interest of their purse.
They mourn the loss of wealth, more than decline of health.
I hate them for their greediness.

PEDROLDA.—These rascals covet e'en the little we possess.
The inquisition should exterminate them all.

LUDOVICO.—We have commenced a new crusade,
To consecrate it in the Hebrews' blood——
Who whistles so infernally as if whole Rome were his.
                        (LEON whistles, without.)
By all the blessed ave-marys—it is a Ribbon-peddler.
What say'st thou Pedrolda to this lucky chance?
Ah, the virgin never does forget her faithful servants.
Let me count my money—only one hundred ducats;——
Wilt thou loan me what thou hast about thee?
I will return it all with thanks.

PEDROLDA.—At any other time, brother Ludovico.
Pedrolda means to trade those ribbons in.

LUDOVICO.—The devil thou dost.
I do intend to buy them all.

PEDROLDA.—I tell thee, brother Ludovico: I 'll have my
        share,
Or else I 'll give assistance none to carry off
The black-eyed damsel we espied last night.

LUDOVICO.—What! dost thou mean to threaten me?
I 'll have thee burnt for stealing to a virgin's bed.

PEDROLDA.—Cease quarreling, my good brother, cease.
Denying thee assistance to abduct yon maid,
Would be indeed as profitless to me,
As burning on the stake thy friend, would be to thee:
For what one loses the other does not gain.
So let 's make peace and jointly purchase up,
All what the noisy Ribbon-Peddler has for sale.

LUDOVICO.—So be it then ;—reach out thy money.
We will accost him as he comes along.
(*Enter* LEON whistling; with gay Ribbon-strings tied on a long
   staff, which he carries on his shoulders.)
Pedler!—(LEON continues whistling.)   Good evening.

LEON.—A pretty day—a very pretty day, good monks.
I have some handsome ribbons here—all colors.
Look ye! I have the blue, green, purple—ah, purple,
And also white such as the convent sisters use.
(LEON hands o'er the staff, and slowly paces about, whistling.)
  LUDOVICO.—How much an ell for this pearl white?
    (LEON continues with his wretched tune.)
I asked you how much an ell for such as this?
    (LEON grows more noisy with his whistling.)

PEDROLDA.—We ask you the price of this ribbon by the ell.
(LEON turns around, and notices for the first time, that he was
    spoken to.)

LEON.—Very nice ribbons—just from Paris.
(He walks slowly away still whistling the same horrid tune.)

  LUDOVICO.—An aggravating Jew ;—still whistling as if
His life depended on this wretched tune.
A fiery head should have a keener wit
Than his soft skull contains.——Still a whistling.

  PEDROLDA.—We 'll make him pay us for this whistle.

  LEON, (aside.)—Aye, out of your treasury.
    (Continues whistling.)

  LUDOVICO.—Red-headed knave! how much an ell for these?

  LEON.—O, you are speaking to me, holy monks.
I was thinking about brother David ;—ha, ha ;
(Seemingly aside.)   He is the boy ;—he bought mighty cheap
   ribbons.
Bought?—ha-ha; yes on credit—ha-ha-ha.
I 'll sell the ware before his debts fall due.
    (He continues whistling.)

PEDROLDA.—Buy quickly, else the creditors might come.

LEON.—Did you speak to me?

(He turns abruptly to whistling.)

PEDROLDA.—Ludovico; he is void of sense—a lunatic.
These ribbons let us buy—he knows not what they're worth.

LUDOVICO, (taking hold of LEON.)—How much an ell for
  this piece of white?

LEON.—O, yes; this piece—a very nice piece—yes, very
  nice.
I sell not by the ell, but by the string;
These strings are—let me see—four ells long.

(He continues whistling.)

LUDOVICO.—What can we purchase of this cursed fool?
He has no wit to match our sound and tempered mind.
I'll speak to him again, if not successfully—
We'll make him understand what we desire.

LEON.—Did you speak to me?

LUDOVICO.—I did, and mean to have you listen to me too.
Else say you wish to sell no ware, and we will go.
'T is true, these ribbons are not worth the trouble,
But I received an order from the sisterhood,
To which I must attend, although these suit me not.

LEON.—You want to buy? ha-ha; that pleases me.
I thought you but desired to look at them.

LUDOVICO.—Well then, the price for this white string?

LEON.—This single string is worth two ducats if no more.
But holy monks, if you do buy what's here :——
Three hundred do they number 'round this staff—
A pittance only will I have for them;
Thrice two hundred ducats is their cost—
Yet one will satisfy——let none approach.
Look, how fine the silk—is some one coming?

PEDROLDA.—I'll take them all.—Here is the money.

LUDOVICO.—Where is the money?

PEDROLDA.—In thy hands, good brother Ludovico.

LUDOVICO.—Here is the sum demanded, Peddler.—
Put all these ribbons now in order, kind Pedrolda,
Whiles I will see the money counted o'er.

PEDROLDA.—I will.

LUDOVICO, (aside to LEON.)—If you should have more ribbons
 than these here,
I 'll buy them all, but promise none to yonder monk;
Else I will take your license in due time away.
The holy sisters must you first supply,
Who willingly do pay an excellent price.
Bring all you have to No. three in yonder convent,
Thence fetch me soon thy total stock.

LEON.—I promise, holy monk, now fare you well.

LUDOVICO.—I shall depend on you;—Hark! some one
 approaches;
Get you gone.—I 'll see who neareth.
  (LUDOVICO goes to one side to see who comes.)

PEDROLDA, (intercepting LEON.)—Good Jewish friend, a word
 with you.
The balance of your stock I 'll trade for.
Let Ludovico have no more—he hates the Jews.—
Bring thy goods to No. four in yonder convent,
I mean to pay you well for trouble and for ware.
Adieu, he comes.
    (*Exit* LEON.)

LUDOVICO.—Look! The Jew of Saxony comes here.
We 'll show him what we bargained for,
And have him give his honest thoughts to us
About the value of these purchased goods.

PEDROLDA.—I do agree with thee, good brother.
    (*Enter* JOSEPH in a hurry.)

JOSEPH.—Good monks, I'm lost—I know not whence I roam
I'm much tired down, yet am without a resting place.
Would you, dear sirs, inform me if you please,
Where I could lodging find—a clean restaurant.

LUDOVICO.—We'll show you such, if you will walk with us;
But ere we go—please answer what we ask:
These ribbons here we bought before you came;
Of various colors is this lot as you perceive—
How much, in honest faith, think you they're worth?

PEDROLDA.—Examine well, kind Hebrew friend,
For in your judgment will we satisfaction find.

JOSEPH.—Since you desire it, friends, I'll value them.
Let me see—three hundred strings they count;—
I should suppose their worth one thousand ducats;
At least I'd pay that sum for such a lot.

LUDOVICO.—'T is just the sum we paid in cash,
But still since you in hunt for such do seem,
We'll spare you, sir, this lot, as we can get another such.

JOSEPH.—A thousand thanks, most holy sirs; a thousand
thanks.
But to avail myself of this, your boundless generosity,
I shall be forced to trouble you somewhat,
With these two drafts of twice five hundred ducats.
They are to our great House in Saxony,
From whence returns are made immediately.

LUDOVICO.—They answer just as well as silver coin.
Have you endorsed upon the back?

JOSEPH.—They are drawn up in mine own name;
As you can see I signed them over.   But now,
Please show me where you think it best to lodge,
And if you more such bargains know to get,
For me, if you desire them not, pray purchase them.
Come now, most holy friend, for I am tired.

Exit JOSEPH, LUDOVICO, and PEDROLDA.

51

SCENE 4th.—AN APARTMENT IN THE CLOISTER.
Present— *Cornelia and Benjamin.*

BENJAMIN.—I 'm tired of singing, sister, I crave some little
rest.

CORNELIA.—Repeat it, sweetest Benjamin, repeat it for my
sake ;
A double charm thine innocence weaves 'round the tune.
If Jephthah loved the song : O, let it live in thee,
And warble forth the ditty while I calmly list.
The nightingales will swell their voices to thy tune,
And leave the boughs they hallowed with their notes.
The chirping lark who wakes the slumbering day,
And greets the rosy morn with sacred melody,
Deserts her field to hear thy mellow voice.
O ! then rehearse his love in gentle strains to me,
Whiles I call up the past to crown it with my tears.

BENJAMIN.—To please thee, sister, I 'll repeat the song,
Which Jephthah in a happier mood oft chimed.
Of late, methought, he sang it in a manner wild ;
His clarion-voice rose from a fount of sighs,
Still dripping with the pearls it scattered to the winds,
Till nature's echo answered to his wild complaint.
Large tears would then shoot forth in little waves,
The which he quickly dried, whene'er some one came near.

CORNELIA.—And I the cause as well as causer of those tears.
Oh ! wretched misery, to be a miserable wretch ;—
A living wretch consigns all joy to death ;
Dead joy surrounds the virgin in yon skies ;
The skies proclaim her welcome in my misery.
O Saint ! let bliss escape from yon high vault,
And may it soothe my Jephthah's blighted hopes,
Whose wretchedness I caused in thy behalf.

BENJAMIN.—Cease grieving, sister, cease.—Jehovah loves
the good.
Thy face is sweet—thy ways are mild and mannerly.

I 'm sure I see no reason for thy sorrows.
These monks who brought me here are very wicked men——
No baser men on earth. Have they been wronging thee?

CORNELIA.—Thou must not call them wicked men. Fie, fie!
These monks are holy men—they serve our sainted virgin.—
Now, boy, begin thy song. Here sit thee by my side.

BENJAMIN.—SONG.

Hear, O hear! thy lover calls:
    Leave, maid, leave thy lonely bower;
He ascendeth now yon walls,
    Coming to thee in the tower;
Haste thee, haste thee, gentle bride,
        Gentle bride;
Love will guide thee in thy flight,
        In thy flight.

Stars are gleaming brightly now,
    Whiles the moon reveals her face;
Come, then come, and plight thy vow
    In thy lover's fond embrace.
Look, he scales the turret's hight,
        Turret's hight;
Dark his look, as dark as night,
        Dark as night.

From the lattice down the rocks,
    Leaps he in the sea below;
Gory shake his raven locks,
    Nightly on the river Po.
Perjured maid, his ghost is here,
        Ghost is here;
Claiming thee, to fill his bier,
        Fill his bier.

CORNELIA.—Break off thy song—I can not hear the rest.
A horrid spectre flits around my melancholic eye,
With streams of blood besmearing all it meets;—

And now—oh! no—not wolves and jackals:
Look! they're after Jephthah—they want his blood—
Keep off—O, tear him not to pieces—
Let him live—he is too young to die.
Holy mother! they have—they have killed him.

    BENJAMIN.—What ails thee, sister? thou dost fright me
      much;
O, tell me how I may assistance give.
A deadly pallor sweeps across thy brow;
Unnatural fire shoots through thy restless eyes.
What shall I do?—I'm at a loss for help.
What? sister, what?—here rest thy head awhile;
'Tis only little Benjamin, the novice.

    CORNELIA.—I'm calm, sweet youth;—ring for the prioress.
              (BENJAMIN rings a bell.)
    BENJAMIN.—What terrified thee, sister?
    CORNELIA.—A trifle, a mere trifle;—these flowers fetch, I
      pray.
Perhaps the scent will do me good.
How sweet; and yet how soon they'll waste away.
Take them again; I am relieved somewhat.

    BENJAMIN.—O, may'st thou ne'er feel unhappy more.
To see thee suffer is a sorry sight to me.
My trust in God should well support all pain,
Yet weep I must, when grief tries thy infirmities.

    CORNELIA.—Blessed is the mother to call thee her own flesh;
Blessed is the sire diffusing pity in thy heart;
Blessed is the hearth that was to thee a temple;
Blessed is the world while thou art part of her.
That part, may it continue in its happy growth,
Until thy virtues purify the misled earth.

    BENJAMIN.—Praised be the tongue to bless my mother so;
Blessed be the heart that spoke my father's praise;
Happy be thy home to call his household pure;
Pure be thy life to make thy prayer heard.

6

CORNELIA.—Amen.

BENJAMIN.—Amen, my mother with uplifted eyes repeats,
When father blessings gives to Jephthah and to me.
We then would rise to kiss my parents' brow,
Who in return relate the sufferings of our race,
To teach us be content by keeping down our eyes;
Nor teach us look too high, else falling hurts the more.

CORNELIA.—If wisdom such is common with thy race,
More needs our church the humbled Hebrews' love,
Than inquisitions to exterminate who practice it.
But tell, dear child, is Jephthah versed in these?

BENJAMIN.—Thou shouldst but hear when he of justice
    speaks.
He reasons boldly, yet listens to superior minds;
If of his wrong convinced, he nobly does acknowledge it.
If right—he stops their praises short. But if
Injustice pleads, uninterrupted follows he
The reptile to his end, to make him swallow,
Step by step, the venom he threw up.
Then foaming anger knits his lofty brow,
And through the ridges courses fiery blood;
His chest dilates; his voice to thunder grows;
His eye-balls deeper in their hollow sockets sink,
And sinking blazes bold defiance forth.

CORNELIA.—Has he no pity for the erring wretch?

BENJAMIN.—None, sister, none, unless he does repent.

CORNELIA.—Is he so stern?

BENJAMIN.—He's stern to such, but kind to those he loves.
He is not harsh, but has a warm and tender heart;
Nor adds he ruthless insult to reproof,
But weeps when others greet him with abuse.
Some christian maid has caused him bitter tears,
For I did watch him close, when he one night came home,
Telling mother how she sneered at his proposal,

And wounded his kind heart in thinking it debased.
He then did weep—I saw it with mine eyes.

CORNELIA.—And did he love the maid?

BENJAMIN.—He loved her better than his life, I'm sure.
When father questioned him about her worth,
He smiled and answered in his glowing tongue,
That mortal can't describe an angel well.
She is a sister like thyself, but not as good,
For thou, I know, wouldst love him at first sight.

CORNELIA.—What makes thee think so, child?

BENJAMIN.—I well remember that my teacher said,
The qualities we lack, in others we admire;
If this be so my cousin wouldst thou love:
For he is gay as April hours without their fickleness;
While thou art calm as summer eves, but far more changeable;
He is as wild and jovial as the fork-horned roe,—
Thou tamer than the petted turtle-dove;
His voice is clamorous like the thunderbolt,—
Thine, milder than the zephyrs playing with thy cheeks;
I know him strong and fearless as the bull,—
Thou wouldst compare well with the timid hare;
He has base enemies, but boldly braves them all,—
Thou art with holy sisters, yet shadows frighten thee;
And then his form, a type of strength and lofty majesty,—
Whiles thine is emblem of sweet thoughts and suffering holi-
     ness.
His eyes are dark and flash commanding eloquence,
Whiles in thy sockets sky-born mildness weeps.
His raven curls impress his features with subdueless fortitude,
But instability peeps through the ringlets of thy golden hair.
Like lilies twined with pinks and roses in a wreath,
Thy virtues would appear linked to his qualities.

CORNELIA.—Well hast thou drawn his picture, child.
This holy kiss be thy reward.   (She kisses him.)

BENJAMIN.—Knowest thou, my cousin Jephthah?

CORNELIA.—I do, sweet child;—I know him, ah, too well.

BENJAMIN.—Thou dost? and lovest him not?

CORNELIA.—Love him not?—O, virgin!—not love him?
Ask the bleeding heart and it will answer:
Love stabbed me to the core.—Ask the milkless breast,
A sigh escapes her then.—Ask the hollow cheeks,
And paleness flits across the burning brow.—O!
Ask these mournful eyes, and they will shed a sea of tears.
Ask the bending form—these tottering steps,
And woman cries: love crippled them. Love him?
O heart! burst not thy tender rills, else pity
At this sight would freeze the blood and turn it white.
Do I love him? O, virgin! virgin! it maddens me!

    BENJAMIN.—He would return this love, were he to see thy
      face.

    CORNELIA.—Never will he see my face again.

    BENJAMIN.—Art thou the woman who made light of him?

    CORNELIA.—The woman worships what the convent-sister
      spurned;
And I am she, who wronged him so.—But come;
Give me a kiss, for now we part eternally.—
I hear the footstep of the prioress. She has
An order to hand thee to the Capuchins,
Who will instruct thee in their holy rites.

    BENJAMIN.—Why part eternally?—I oft
Will come to speak and sing to thee.

    CORNELIA.—They will not let thee; or if they would,
My vow will keep me from receiving thee.

    BENJAMIN.—What vow is this thou speak'st of sister?

    CORNELIA.—An oath I took when I did join the sisterhood.
To stay, till death, secluded in this nunnery,
And think no more of earth as if I were not on't.
To meet no friends, save such who are like me,
Pure virgins wretched in their chastity. If holy men

Have business with the prioress, our faces
We must cover well, that while they speak,
They may our features not perceive, nor we their own.

BENJAMIN.—Cravest thou no further liberties?

CORNELIA.—The holy virgin grants no more.

BENJAMIN.—I do not understand thee well, or if I do:
Explain to me I pray, how Jephthah came,
To meet thee in the nunnery, and meeting thee,
Behold thy face uncovered.   For so, he must,
Else could he not extol thy virtues and thy beauty so.

CORNELIA.—Am I so beautiful?

BENJAMIN.—Thou art, sweet sister; I do not flatter.

CORNELIA.—I wish I were not so.

BENJAMIN.—Thou knowest not what thou sayest;
For God does love the beautiful.

CORNELIA.—Not all the beautiful are virtuous.

BENJAMIN.—But all the virtuous are beautiful.
For all the tender passions—the nobler thoughts—
The generous disposition—self-sacrificing love;
All these—intrinsic beauties stamp upon the brow,
To modify the defects externally perceived.

CORNELIA.—Who has instructed thee so well?

BENJAMIN.—O, sister dear, I am ashamed to be so ill advised.
Had Jephthah studied half the wisdom of my sire,
And I picked up the half of the neglected half,
Both would be wiser by the half of half I left,
The whole and more of what we jointly know.

CORNELIA.—Thy years lack pace to keep up with thy mind.

BENJAMIN.—I know no more than any Hebrew child.

CORNELIA.—If Jewish children be so wise, how great must
be their sires?

BENJAMIN.—More useful to the world, than Roman inquisitions.
6*

CORNELIA.—What knowest thou of the holy inquisition?

BENJAMIN.—But little yet; I crave to learn no more.
They threatened me with some dire cruelties.

CORNELIA.—Who could be so unmerciful?

BENJAMIN.—The inquisitors who dragged me here —
Ludovico and Pedrolda.

CORNELIA.—Why have they menaced thee, poor child?

BENJAMIN.—Last night it was—some little after dark,
When yonder bells pealed forth the hour of Mass,
And people congregated in the chapel then,
To read Ave-marys and some Pater-nosters.
I, as desired, attended service with the prioress,
Where I strange things perceived to make me smile withal,
But not, unhappy nun, as much at what they prayed,
As at their superstition shown by the following:
A string of shining beads—they called a rosary—
Each in his fingers with odd reverence held;
And after closing an ave-mary—for so methinks
They style the prayer—a single bead they'd take
To slip it on one side. At every prayer's close,
A single pearl was moved until they counted ten;
And then a Pater-noster was delivered up,
The end of which was marked by joining a large bead
To the preceding ten of smaller size, and so kept on
Until at last they chimed a Gloria-Patri——
Which as they taught me here—means " Praise
To God," the Father. Just then those monks I so abhor,
Approached my pew and gave to me a rosary,
Commanding me to follow the example shown :
To pray Ave-marys through one whole decade.
I then, refusing to become apostate to my God,
Whom I upon my mother's breast was taught to love ;
And knowing I'd displease my father with the change,
In so forgetting what he trained me to believe :
To worship but one God, and He, the God of Israel.—

They then did threaten me with cruelties unheard,
The which, I thought, were meant to frighten me.
But as I saw their purple lips in anger quiver,
Disclosing—O, such teeth! they wolf-like gnashed on me,
I then began to weep—their faces bespoke their earnestness.
(*Enter* PRIORESS and LAWRENCE.)

PRIORESS.—Come, holy father come; the Hebrew boy is
here.

LAWRENCE.—Peace to thy soul, good sister, peace.

CORNELIA.—Amen. Be comfort thine, good Lawrence.

LAWRENCE.—Amen.

CORNELIA.—Father! what great cause engages thy good
work?

LAWRENCE.—It is the sacred Pontiff's mighty will, this boy
From thy good care to take and place him with
The Capuchins.

PRIORESS.—His holy majesty shall be obeyed.

CORNELIA.—Benjamin, come hither, Benjamin.

LAWRENCE.—The holy sister calls thee, boy.

CORNELIA.—Benjamin.

PRIORESS.—Why dost not answer; child?

BENJAMIN.—What wilt thou, sister?

CORNELIA.—Bid thee, farewell, my child.
This gentle friar means to take thee hence.

BENJAMIN.—Well.—Come, come.

PRIORESS.—Take first my blessing, child.
We love thee.—May the virgin ever smile on thee.

BENJAMIN.—Come, Friar.

LAWRENCE.—By the sainted Mary! thou art in haste.

CORNELIA.—Benjamin.

BENJAMIN.—Sister.

CORNELIA.—Art angry?—fear not, sweet child, fear not.

BENJAMIN.—Fear? O, my father, mother, your child weeps.

CORNELIA.—Thou leavest with a heavy heart.

BENJAMIN.—Heavy?

CORNELIA.—Why art thou sparing with thy words?

BENJAMIN.—Come, friar. (*Exit* BENJAMIN.)

LAWRENCE.—He fears to leave ye, sisters.

CORNELIA.—He does dislike this Ludovico, much.
I pity this poor child.

PRIORESS.—Fie, fie; Cornelia; although severe,
The holy Benedictines know their office.

CORNELIA.—O, virgin! grant me pardon.

PRIORESS.—Amen.

CORNELIA.—Strange, how this poor child affliction wears;
Without a murmur from his infant lips,
He weeps the loss of home which well preserved his innocence,
Still blessing every inmate of its sacred shrine,
From whence he ruthlessly was dragged away.

LAWRENCE.—I pity him with all my heart.
His sufferings commence but now.
The church demandeth many sacrifices.

CORNELIA.—Frail humans as we are; we pity what we must
approve.

PRIORESS.—Let's keep our entire faith, in Father, Son,
And Holy Ghost.—Offend them not,
By searching for the wisdom of those sacred laws,
Our understanding has no right to penetrate.

LAWRENCE.—We dare not doubt the virtue of the Roman
Law.
Let it suffice, our holy Pontiff knows them just.
It is our duty to obey.

CORNELIA.—I comply with his desires. His will is mine.

LAWRENCE.—In meekness let us serve the church.

CORNELIA.—How willingly! could she but keep the passions
    quiet;
Good friar, kindly treat this boy.
I pray thee, do.

LAWRENCE.—I would, were it within my power.
But Ludovico, the Inquisitor,
Will henceforth have the charge o'er him.

PRIORESS.—Since thou dost mention Ludovico's name,
I recollect the holy Pontiff's words through him:
It is his will, to give thee audience, sister,
To-morrow when he has his sacred court.

CORNELIA, (aside.)—To have my audience?

PRIORESS.—Prepare to meet the Pontiff.—One chaplet
Read this night—no less at dawn.
Now brother, let us to this boy attend;
The holy fathers, will be here ere long.
        (*Exit* PRIORESS.)

LAWRENCE.—Take my benediction, sister.   (He blesses her.)
May peace attend thee here.

CORNELIA.—Amen.
        (*Exit* LAWRENCE.)

Peace to me?
O, Jephthah, why didst ever cross my path?—
Why do I love thee?—I was happy ere I knew thee,
But now—wretched—miserable—wicked.
And yet I would not wipe thee from my memory,
For all the bliss to heavenly angels granted.
What wants his holy majesty?—his life?
Must I accuse him?—O, what sufferings!
What bitter—bitter sufferings!—accuse him?
Never, never!—holy virgin, I put my trust in thee.
I'll save him—what matters it if I be cursed?—
I love him and can not—can not help it.
I am a woman and must love.
        (*Exit* CORNELIA.)

SCENE 5th.—IN FRONT OF THE CONVENT.

Enter LEON with Ribbons, and LUDOVICO.

LEON.—You then received the note I left
In your apartment?

LUDOVICO.—I have, most honest peddler.
But had you stayed ten minutes longer,
You could have saved yourself this trouble.
I only went to see the holy prioress.

LEON.—I would have waited for your coming,
But—is no one near?—but—

LUDOVICO.—But—

LEON.—To continue. As I approached the convent,
Then thinking unperceived—look around—

LUDOVICO.—I will, mine honest peddler.

LEON.—My brother's creditors did follow me.
Of me they had no right to claim the things
I bought and paid for.—I love honesty.

LUDOVICO.—I know you do.

LEON.—Come this way.—I then
Did hide in your apartment for awhile.

LUDOVICO.—Give me your hand, most honest peddler.
I thought you were deceiving me.

LEON.—I do not understand you.

LUDOVICO.—I will be candid with you, peddler.
Know then, I did behold you going to the convent
When business of importance took me to the prioress.
And as I hurried home to meet you as appointed,
Methought I heard you in Pedrolda's room,
Persuading him to purchase what you had.
Then angry at myself I entered mine own room,
Where I your short epistle first espied.
To read its brief contents was but a moment's work,
Assuring me but half way of your honesty.
Still fearing you had dealt at No. four,'

I had Pedrolda to confirm those lines,
After which I left to meet you here.

LEON.—Adieu.——I well perceive
You have no confidence in me.

LUDOVICO.—Stay.—
I acknowledge the wrong of suspecting you.
You stopped in my apartment.—Continue.

LEON.—And so I did to hide my ware;
Then went to meet those men—they greeted me.
Of course I kindly welcomed them. We spoke
On various topics, until at last I hinted
Of my brother's prospering affairs—how much
He gained of late—his intention to enlarge
The business he so prospers in—well.
I left them satisfied with what they heard,
And I returned to get my Ribbons then.—
Do you want to purchase these articles?

LUDOVICO.—The lot I bought, I could not use at all;—
The sisterhood wants better—yes, better ware.

LEON.—The goods I have will prove superior to the last.
Since you complain—I'll offer you no more.
I understand a Saxon has arrived in Rome,
Who offers better prices than you paid me.
I'll find him out, perhaps he'll trade with me.

                    (He tries to go off.)

LUDOVICO.—Be not too hasty, peddler. Ludovico keeps his
    word.
Since I have promised——

LEON.—I will release you of your promise.

LUDOVICO.—But the holy virgin won't.—Then stay.
All I will claim is fairer dealing than before,
As an equivalent for my boundless confidence in you.

LEON.—Well, upon my word—upon mine honest word,
You are a gentleman; yes, a noble gentleman;

Yet I'll accept no more generosity of you,
Than I can thankfully make up in trade,
To show you my appreciation for your kindness.

LUDOVICO.—'Tis well.—I will believe your word.
Now show the goods the holy sisters need.

LEON.—Yet ere I further in this trade advance,
This much I will explain to you, good monk;
These Ribbons all I'll sell or none,
I would not break the lot could I for half
Get almost what the whole is worth.
The Saxon merchant buys assorted stocks.

LUDOVICO.—For this transaction, peddler, I prepared myself.
If you're right cheap with this assortment here,
We can the bargain close with difficulties none.

LEON.—I hope we may.
This stock embraces—look—two thousand strings;
Each single one three ducats costs.
In short six thousand ducats is the aggregate amount.
Now if you feel inclined my silks to buy,
Two thousand ducats will I take for all.

LUDOVICO.—Too much, too much, for such a lot as this.
I'll give you eighteen hundred, if you'll accept of them.

LEON.—I can not take one farthing less, my friend.
But still I'll tell you what I mean to do:
This Saxon merchant will I hunt up first,
And if he offers me no more than you have done,
Why then, of course, the ribbons shall be yours.

LUDOVICO.—If you expect to get a better price than mine,
You mean to get more than the goods are worth.
Besides the Saxon merchant left this morn;
To Paris have I heard it said, he went.

LEON.—Are you sure it was the Saxon,
Who left our city?

LUDOVICO.—I'm certain of the fact; but still,

If nothing less will do—your price receive.
The sisters will forgive me for mine casiness.

LEON.—Two thousand ducats I demand.

LUDOVICO.—Here is the sum.

LEON.—I thank you, holy monk.
One favor I would beg of you—

LUDOVICO.—If in my power, I will grant it to you.

LEON.—These ribbons, please, let no one but the sisters see ;
As I have foes—you know what foes might do.
See! Pedrolda moves this way—adieu.

LUDOVICO.—Adieu.—If you should ever see him,
Acquaint him not with this our speculation.

Exit LEON.

These ribbons will I hide.—He need not know
That I have traded with the Jew.—Let me count:
By the virgin! these two thousand strings,
At least ten thousand ducats will they fetch.
What! give Pedrolda half?—no—not I.
He comes; I must conceal these ribbons.

(*Exit* LUDOVICO.)

Enter PEDROLDA with Ribbons.

PEDROLDA.—If I can get five ducas for one string,
Ten thousand will this lot of ribbons bring.
Pedrolda! more dignity;—Pedrolda!
More honor.—Pedrolda! you are a made man.
Shall Ludovico share my fortune ?—never.
Not a farthing shall he have—the upstart.
I can become a bishop now—a holy bishop.

Exit PEDROLDA.

SCENE 6TH.—THE HEBREWS' BURYING PLACE.

Enter Rabbi, preacher & Off. in procession; the corpse of Yulah; Mortara, Jephthah, Abraham, Judah, followed by six youths in mourning; Rifka and six virgins, wearing white garments with garlands 'round their brows, which they keep covered until the commencement of the song. A strain of low and mournful music at the distance, which dies away as soon as all the mourners are on the stage.

RABBI.—Set down the coffin.—Come, chief mourners, come,
The corpse once more behold. The spirit
Still lingers near the clay it tenanted. Let it
Not soar on High with the wrongs ye heaped on it.
(MORTARA kneels in front of the coffin; to his right Jephthah
and Judah; to his left, Rifka and Abraham.)

MORTARA.—If e'er in thine incarnate life we wronged thee,
Spirit! we beg thy pardon. Forgive; O,
Make us happy. As thou expectest Heavenly mercy
From the all-wise Judge, who in His arms
Will soon enfold thee: forgive thy grieving household.
If I ever for a moment wronged thee, Spirit!
Or caused one tear to flow—one sigh to escape—
Or was guilty of harsh language—of untender words:
As I hope to meet thee shortly in an everlasting embrace,
Aye, from my heart I do repent. O, spirit!
Grant me pardon, who bowed down with silver-age
Hath ever studied thine own happiness. And if
I sometimes failed in my ceaseless efforts: ascribe
It not to my suffering soul. Forgive me, Spirit!
If thou lovest to linger o'er the past when thou and I
Were children; yet plucking daisies and forget-me-nots,
To weave garlands for each other's infant-brow—
If thou lovest to remember when I called thee, wife,
Leading thee from the altar gently to my home;
Realizing all the bliss the yearning heart engendered—
Where thou didst pledge to bear my weaknesses,
And be a faithful partner unto me:—by the memory
Of these happy hours I implore thee to forgive.

In the name of thy son—our Benjamin—
I appeal to thee to pardon his sire. Let peace
And love exist 'tween thee and me—'tween thee
And thy household—'tween thee and Israel.
(MORTARA and mourners arise.)

ALL.—Amen.

RABBI.—Swerving soul! break loose thy ties on earth;
   (He takes some earth and throws it into the coffin.)
May'st thou dead corse soon moulder into dust.
(He retires quickly, and so one after another throws some
       earth into the coffin, retiring quickly)
The spirit fled—proclaim its flight!
(Trumpets within.)

MORTARA.—Almighty father! Holy and immaculate God!
Thou, who daily shower'st blessings on thy creatures,
And in Thy mercy pardonest them for their trespasses,
Behold me in submission bend my knees.—O,
Hear thy feeble servant addressing Thee:
Claim, O Father! the undefiled spirit of my Yulah,
And have compassion with her soul.—Receive
Her in Thy mighty arms and show her Grace
And Charity.—For her sins, O just Jehovah,
Let on Thy supplicating servant fall Thy wrath.
Fill full my cup of sorrow—I'll drink the last dregs,
Until I expiated for her actions disapproved.
Open wide the portals of Heaven—acquaint
The angels of an absent spirit returning to its home.
Receive it in Thy mercy, and let it
Shine on High.—Creator of this mighty universe!
Hear mine appeal and take her soul to Heaven.

ALL.—Amen.

SONG BY THE VIRGINS.

Though with angels in heaven thou art smiling,
Where Jehovah is keeping thee near,
And thy wit be no longer beguiling——
Yet thy mem'ry we bless and revere,
Yet thy mem'ry we bless and revere,

When gentle and lovely thy face,
The tears from the cheeks did erase :
    We blessed thy good heart—
        Sang loudly thy praise ;
        Such garlands to guard,
            To vie with thy gaze.
Not a star in yon sky so bright,
But can borrow from thee some light.
No, no !—not a star in yon sky is so bright——
            Is so bright.

Though the widows and orphans be weeping,
    For the hand that has fed them lies low ;
Yet they're happy to know thou art reaping,
    The reward for thy pity below—
    The reward for thy pity below.
In the spring when the flowers bloom,
We will cover with daisies thy tomb ;
        As pure was thy love,
            And purer thy thought,
        Now reigning above,
            A pleasure to God.
Not a creature on earth so small,
But with tears didst thou mourn his fall——
No, no !—not a creature on earth was too small—
            Was too small.

When the meadows begin to be flowing,
    Like a streamlet o'ershaded with green ;
Then with songs we will come to the wooing,
    To the dreamland we never have seen—
    To the dreamland we never have seen.
In yon vault of bright stars abide ;
We will watch thee appear to-night.
        We love the blue sky,
            Where spirits in glee,
        Catch quickly the sigh,
            Escaping from thee.
When the nightingales ring the air
We will come to thee where—O, where ?
Yes, yes ;—we will come when the nightingales ring—
            When the nightingales ring.
    (The curtain drops with the last repetition.)
        Exeunt.——[*End of 2d Act.*]

ACT THIRD.

Scene 1st.—In Front of the Convent.

Enter Ludovico.

Ludovico.—Fooled; by the virgin, fooled;—Ludovico's
    fooled.

This Saxon merchant—ha, ha—Saxon merchant—
A damned Jew, who lives by his thieving wit,
Did so excite me with this ribbon-speculation,
That all my thoughts were fixed upon this theme,
Which blended me with dreams of wealth—of gold,
To keep me from suspecting this bold roguery.
What can I do with the goods?—nothing.
I can not sell these printed cotton-strings;—
Where was my mind?—my usual judgment,
To think this fancy trash, the best of silken ware?
The dealers say: two ducats is about their worth.
Two ducats—and I gave two thousand for them.
Was ever man so cheated?—so duped?
Two thousand ducats for two ducats worth of goods.
O, red-headed Jew let me but find thee——
Ha-ha-ha—find him?—he is too keen to stay.
By the virgin! I perceive it—why, 'tis plain:
The Saxon and the peddler were colleagued.
They understood each other—devised this plan;——
All, all, to swindle Ludovico.—I looked for him,
At the house to which I recommended him——
Who would think it! he never passed the threshold.
No, by the virgin, no!—they never saw the man.
Shall I stand this imposition?—suffer it?
I shall have the cheat proclaimed.—Stop—
Halt awhile, Ludovico;—will they not laugh
To see thee so outdone?—where is thy pride?—
Can I do nothing to get rid of these goods?
Diddle for diddle is an even barter.
Let me see—I have it—Pedrolda must share half.
I will divide with him, and make him pay his part.
    7*

But how manage it?—I vowed the peddler went from Rome,
And ceased to deal in ware;—let me think awhile.
Yes, this will do and keep suspicion quiet. Good.
I'll make him think,—as he upbraided me,—
Aye, suspected me of having privily received the Jew—
That for his sake I bought these ribbons.
So I one thousand ducats will receive at least,
And let the other pay me for excess of greediness.
Ludovico, thou art wise,—this folly hide within thy breast,
Hence learn to eat but what thy stomach can digest.

(*Exit* LUDOVICO.)

*Enter six Benedictines, each in his usual habiliment of a loose, grey
gown, with wide and open sleeves and wearing a pointed cowl; Pope
Pius, Cardinal Savelli, Bishop Bedini, followed by Pedrolda and
six Benedictines. Music within.*

PIUS.—With arms uplifted lay he at our feet;
His voice in trembling accents to us came——
But what of that? Savelli! our heart is steeled;
Ten thousand wrongs heaped on ten thousand more,
Each penetrating into the lacerated bosom
Ten thousand times more deep than his did pierce,
Affects not us.—Stern is our nature.
On, good Benedictines, to the room of State;
Apprise the ecumenical council of our approach.

(*Exit* BENEDICTINES; PIUS stops PEDROLDA.)

Good monk, we have some business with thee.

PEDROLDA.—Your Holy Grace needs but to command.

PIUS.—'Tis well.
And thought he to move us with his tears?
Find us wavering and release the boy?
To stay the threatening arm and deal out mercy?—
Expected he—Prelates! we'll not give under.
No! by St. Peter, no!—like as the deluge of old
In one mighty whirlpool choked revolting earth,
So shall our hate in pestilential vapors rise
Huge clouds of death to taint the face of life,

And sweep the new-born infant, Liberty, to Hell,
And all who would promote its growth against our will.
What says our brother, cardinal?

SAVELLI.—Far less, most Holy Grace, since your great mind
Confounded well my little wit.—We can not fail.

BEDINI.—We will succeed——

PIUS.—Will?—will? ha, ha;—must!—our will proclaims it;
The Pope must sway the world, or sink with it;
We're tired of half-way doings—it courteth fear.
What! have we degenerated?—become effeminate?
No! by the holy Peter, no!—Rome disputes it to the world!
The council meets to-day—let's well observe its mien.
The envoys speak their master's mind—we'll drink each word;
Revolt broods at our court—it must be suppressed—
By fine strokes of policy—with fire and steel—
By any means to stab the Protestantic cause.
The boy shall never see Mortara more,
Though all Europe should appeal.   What!
If England should be threatening!—France, wavering!
We'll teach them obedience to the Roman-church.
No, brothers, no—we dare so long we have a voice.
Let Aeneas with brave Hector join the fray—
Yet Troy must fall and Ilion lose her sway.
Come Prelates—
(To Pedrolda:) Inform sister Cornelia, our Grace would see
   . her.
Come to the council.

(*Exit* POPE, CARDINAL and BISHOP.)

PEDROLDA.—The inquisitors will have some work at last,
And Hebrew blood shall flow in mighty rivers forth.—
But this brings not the Saxon back to me,
To rid me of those ribbons I have bought.
I begin to smell a rat.—Peddler and Saxon left,—
The devil take them;—by the holy mother!
'Tis plain—plain as day: and I did not see it.

They were co-partners in this trade to swindle me.
I wonder what the ribbons can be worth?
Who knows!—I fear me I'm badly chiseled.
I wonder what the ribbons can be worth?—
I'll inquire at the dealers—they can inform me best.
Since no one's here, I may as well peruse this letter.

(He takes a letter from his pocket and reads it.)

As I said.—Swindled, as I said;—no money to his credit?
The drafts sent back unpaid, he being unknown to the firm?
I'll have police-men after him—the scoundrel.
Think to cheat the holy monk Pedrolda.—
What's best to do?—show this letter to Ludovico?
No, certainly, not.—He must not know of it.
I'll haste to him straight and bargain him the ware.
I'll keep him in the dark with what I now suspect.
That's smart;—Pedrolda thou art not quite a fool;
For wiser men have been the Hebrews' tool.

Enter LUDOVICO.

LUDOVICO.—My holy brother!
Pedrolda, I'm delighted to see thee.

PEDROLDA.—Kindest Ludovico! dost know I ever cared for
thee?

LUDOVICO.—I am assured of thy most generous disposition,
Which well befits thy station as a holy father;
The poor have found thee e'er their benefactor,
And all who know thee praise thy virtues high.
I, therefore, in appreciation of thy merits,
Have made thee rich, my faithful partner,—rich.

PEDROLDA.—Wise and worthy friend, here take my hand.
Of all the Benedictines none loves thee more than I.
To prove these words I sealed them with a deed,
Regardless of mine own advantages.

LUDOVICO.—I'm sure, no selfish motive influences thee,
But holy thoughts incite and move thy will.
We labor here to gain a happier life beyond.

Our Savior promised and thou wilt enjoy.
What's gold to me, unless my friends enjoy its benefit?

PEDROLDA.—'Tis even so; we can not take it hence;
And yet we need it here for holy purposes,
Which being used in this approved manner:
To build up churches and maintain their functionaries—
Establish inquisitions and their secret spies:
Will make us happy in the means to do it with.

LUDOVICO.—I therefore made thee partner in all trades,
Which promise profit and advance our happiness.

PEDROLDA.—And I accepted then thy proffered love.

LUDOVICO.—In mutual friendship let us share our wealth,
And all the profits by our trades accruing.

PEDROLDA.—In concert to thy wish have I, to please thee,
    dealt;
And bought two thousand ducats worth of ware:
The half of which I charged to thy account.

LUDOVICO.—The devil thou didst.

PEDROLDA.—Thou needst not be angry with thy friend;
I am not selfish and thou shalt know it.
The total sum I mean to charge thee with,
Since thou prefer'st to own the complete stock.
I won't hear thy thanks—thy acknowledgments.

LUDOVICO.—Pedrolda!—thou art mad.

PEDROLDA.—I assure thee that void of envy, I resigned it.

LUDOVICO.—Pedrolda!—thou art a fool.

PEDROLDA.—If so, I'll be a kind one.
These ribbons must thou keep.

LUDOVICO.—Why dost thou plague me?—torture me?
Wouldst thou barter some of mine?

PEDROLDA.—Would I?—yes, and thank thy noble heart.

LUDOVICO.—I take thee by thy word, and sell thee all my
    ware.

PEDROLDA.—Hast thou some ribbons too?

LUDOVICO.—I bought one thousand ducats worth for each of us.

PEDROLDA.—The devil thou didst?

LUDOVICO.—The devil I did.—The peddler knows it well.

PEDROLDA.—Did he suck thee as well as me?

LUDOVICO.—He squeezed my pockets dry.

PEDROLDA.—Read these few lines;—from Saxony they came.
(Ludovico reads the letter.)

LUDOVICO.—As I supposed.

PEDROLDA.—Ludovico!

LUDOVICO.—Pedrolda!

PEDROLDA.—Wouldst know what I believe?

LUDOVICO.—What? what dost thou believe?

PEDROLDA.—That our legs convey a pair of donkey-heads.

LUDOVICO.—Thou dost believe so?

PEDROLDA.—I'm almost ashamed to say so;—but I believe it.

LUDOVICO.—Thou art a donkey not to be convinced of it.

PEDROLDA.—Upon my word, I admire thy frankness.

LUDOVICO.—'Tis sure we have been shamefully abused.
But revenge is sweet, and we shall have it soon.

PEDROLDA.—Cornelia's trial comes off to day.
I think the holy Pontiff will soon entrap,
This Hebrew rebel—Mortara's nephew.

LUDOVICO.—I hope he may.—Let's to the council now.

PEDROLDA.—No, no. I to the convent-sister.—So adieu.
Exit PEDROLDA and LUDOVICO.

SCENE 2D.—A HEATH.—THUNDER AND LIGHTNING.
Enter MORTARA and RIFKA.

RIFKA.—O, father come; let's back to Rome again.
Proud Pius past, nor listened to your plaints,

But scoffingly he shoved you to one side,
With threats of death, should you appeal once more.
   (Thunder, lightning and a shower of rain.)
On, father, on; I'll lead you to a home,
Where you can shelter from this tempest's rage
Your silvery head much dripping with this shower.
 Mortara.—Nay, my daughter, nay; here will I couch
  awhile,
And woo the mystic horrors of the elements.
In jarring discord flies their anger forth;
And howling winds shoot through the weeping clouds,
Impregnating each drop with sympathy for me.
Look! the Heaven is shrouded in a gown of grey,
And not a ray emerges through the misty folds,
To warm the earth and melt the hardened heart—
Hear! dost hear the wailing sound, my daughter?
The storm-king chants a requiem o'er dead pity's grave,
And black and dismal clouds pour down their rills,
To wash away the blood still oozing from her wounds.
What will become of me,—old, foolish as I grow,
Since mercy's gone, and pity sleeps beneath a willow-tree.
   (A violent crash of thunder.)
What? I'll ride the storm and wield the thunderbolts;
Sail on the clouds and pour their oceans down;
Let loose the lightning to strike the living, dead.
What shall I do?—nothing, nothing—nothing.
O, tears! flow on; unburthen me withal;
Let your nectarean juce allay the mental heat,
And all the passions settle to a proper state.
   (A shower of rain.)
 Rifka.—Come, father, come; let's seek a friendly hearth,
To harbor us from these inclemencies.
The tempest swells uprooting mighty oaks,
And peals on peals shake earth and make her quiver.
Hyenas and fierce tigers tremble in their lairs,
And feel a fear uncommon to their kind,

Why stay we here? the Pontiff heard us not,
And France and Prussia passed us proudly by;
The envoys all refused to take your grievance in.

MORTARA.—I wait for Austria: he has not passed us yet;
Perhaps he shows more pity than the rest.

RIFKA.—O, hope no mercy from the Austrian hand,
And let us fly from fleers and gibes like his;
With which his railing tongue will greet your ear.
He hates our race and loves to pierce our heart;
To steal our babes and laugh their fathers mad.

MORTARA.—I'll wait for Austria;—he shall hear me.

RIFKA.—Since you resolved to have with Austria speech,
Let's sit on yonder rock, from whose high eminence,
We may espy him as he comes this way.

MORTARA.—Lead me, Rifka.

RIFKA.—I will, kind father.
        (They move back and sit upon the eminence.

LEON, (without.)—Keep thy dishonest gain; I'll none of it.

MORTARA.—What's loose? behold thy brother in an angry
    mood,
Advancing with this outcast reprobate.

RIFKA.—O, separate him from this villain.

MORTARA.—Sit still my daughter for awhile.
            Enter LEON and JOSEPH.

JOSEPH.—'Tis true, thou didst assist me to this wealth,
And well deceivedst those monks as I advised;
Yet think me not so foolish as to share with thee,
Whiles I devised the plan as well as had the ware.

LEON.—I told thee keep thy trash, I'll none of it.

JOSEPH.—I'm willing yet to give thee what I said.

LEON.—But I'm unwilling to accept of it.
Hear, thou enticer to this shameful deed:
Although I fell, I have some virtue in me yet,

To wipe away the shame now tarnishing my brow:
I have disgraced myself to be a villain's tool;
My sire I will not mock in taking aught of thee.
Why did I listen to thy scheming vile!
Wouldst know it, knave? I spake it once before,
Yet I'll repeat it; else thou with turgid vanity,
May'st think me fallen quite so low as thou.
A sister have I, sweet and innocent,
Who claims a brother's vigil, since God took parents hence.
In Italy—O, Italy! we have no home in thee.
Mortara, her protector—the sorrow-stricken sage,
No longer can he guard her blooming years.
And I, too poor to give her such protection,
As the daughter of my father should receive,
Have thought of leaving Rome to seek with her
Columbia's shore, where freedom sails on every breeze—
And her chief magistrates in justice serve the land.
To earn sufficient for this purpose, wretch,
I readily became thine instrument.
But since thou dost refuse the journey's cost,
The which amount was promised to me:
I will not take a farthing of this gain,
And spare the blush to mantle on my cheeks.
I'll not evade the police on our track,
But will resign myself to Rome's tribunal.

       (MORTARA and RIFKA advancing.)

MORTARA.—Hold!

LEON.—What! Mortara here!—my Rifka too!
Why court this boisterous storm?

MORTARA.—Ask not why Mortara braves the tempest's rage,
But hear his words and mark them well.
(To Joseph.) Begone and hide within some distant cave,
And teach the fox the art of pilfering;
Deny thy birth, for Israel claims thee not,
She loathes the spirits who disgrace her so.

       (*Exit* JOSEPH.)

8

O, Leon—Leon, why didst taint thy name?

LEON.—Despise me not, kind sage, 'twas Joseph lured me on.
I craved not wealth, but Rifka's happiness.
I thought of freedom and independency—
The bait was strong; I fell, old man;—
Who would not fall for it?
The dream is o'er and Leon's lost forever.

MORTARA.—Repent, my son; our Father will forgive.
For pleasing in the sight of God is he,
Who from his fall returns to virtue's path,
Outsoaring meekly such who never fell.

LEON.—In prison shall I pay the penalty.
For if I stay, and stay I must in Rome,
They will discover soon my whereabouts,
And doom me hence to drag shame's lineaments.

MORTARA.—Reach me thy hand, daughter;—'tis well.
(He takes a golden chain off his neck and hands it to them.)
Now flee with Rifka to Columbia's shore.
Watch o'er her,—become a better man.
This chain of gold will well defray the cost.
May the God of Israel be your guide.—Go.

RIFKA.—Never, never will I leave you here exposed.
Lonely and alone to wander to and fro.
This golden chain, oh! take it back again,
And keep what you may need, alas! too soon.

LEON.—O, good, old man; you bade my tears come forth;
To see you —— I can not speak—
        (Kneels down and kisses Mortara's hands.)

MORTARA.—Fly, else ye are too late.—Go, my children.
My silver-head —— go, and be happy, go.
            (RIFKA falls before his feet.)

RIFKA.—Mortara, we can not leave you.

MORTARA.—Rise, my children;—go.
            (*Exit* of LEON and RIFKA.)

Strange is the disposition and the fate of man;
And sorrows seem indeed a part of him——
Born in his bosom——reigning in his mind.
Move he where he will—be he where he may,
A certain something nestling in his breast,·
Forever breedeth discontent—unhappiness.
The meek-eyed boy,
Frisking through the tender years of childhood—
Spinning flowers o'er his golden locks—
Catching the rainbow-joys with silvery laughter:
Soon wearies of the same and longs after change.
He weeps, but knows not why he weeps;
Turns peevish, sullen—who can the cause assign?
Hilarious youth—a stranger still to bitter grief,
Madly reeling through the pleasures of the hour,
Draws dreams of bliss from Fancy's inner eye—
Breaks through his chains and panteth after sterner game.
Man—bold, undaunted man—the chief on earth,
Controlling many—obeying but to few—
Enjoying Heaven in a gentle wife's embrace—
Gazing fondly at his prattling babes awhile:
Soon tiring of the scene imbibes ambitious thoughts,
And leaves the hearth and spurns true happiness.
Old age, descending from the rushy stage
Receives the applause and honors of his years:
In weeping after Time—forgets the use of time,
Allotted to him still, and dies a craving wretch.
Thus nature planted imperfection in us all,
And made the passions thwart the purpose of the mind,
Whose happiness is lost in keen desire for more,
Of which possessed, is but as footstool used,
By tramping on the seat whereon to rest,
And move us further from the joys at hand:
Feeling happier in spurning what's acquired,
Than to enjoy and shackle appetite withal.

      (Thunder.)

O, heavenly Father! forgive my soul to grieve;
Excuse the weakness rising in my character.
It was thy will to take my Benjamin;
It is the sire who weeps the loss of him.
I murmur not at what Thy wisdom plans,
But mourn I must.—O, God! how is my boy?
     (Thunder, lightning, followed by a shower of rain.)
Enter AUSTRIA.

Stay your Grace.

AUSTRIA.—Who calls on Austria to halt and drown in rain?
A fool alone expecteth me to stop.

MORTARA.—Be you then wise and calm the wrath of God.

AUSTRIA.—Away, I will not parley with thee now.

MORTARA.—On my knees I beg you to hear my words.

AUSTRIA.—Who art thou, to intercept me thus?

MORTARA.—'Tis I; Mortara the Jew.
[Thunder and lightning.]

AUSTRIA.—(Striking him.) Aback and let me pass.

MORTARA.—Strike me if you will, but hear me speak.

AUSTRIA.—Avaunt; I listen to no Jew.

MORTARA.—O take my grievance in the council room;
His holy grace will favor your appeal.
Release my boy and bless this hoary head.

AUSTRIA.—Much rather pluck these feathers from thy chin.
(He pulls MORTARA's beard, when lightning strikes him dead.)
     (Thunders, lightnings, showers of rain.)

MORTARA.—Ha, ha!—Jehovah is abroad!
Howl on, ye winds! proclaim the heavenly wrath!
Be loud, ye thunders! burst the gates ajar!
Come! shoot a deluge down to sweep the earth!
Put horrid death into the lightning's dart,
And hurl its flame into the stubborn brain,
To craze the few who would escape with life.

(Lightning.)

Flash on, ye fires! revenge my silver crown;
Ride faster, tempest! swell breaths to hurricanes,
And playing zephyrs change into mighty gales.
Frail piece of dust, what art thou now?
Where are thy insults and thy bitter threats?
Still ringing in the air and thou art stayed.
O, trifling worm to think thee powerful withal,
While but a single dart defied thy black intents,
And struck to earth the hand that meant to strike.
Hark! the storm increases—where is my boy?—where?

(He kneels.)

SCENE 3D.—A STREET IN ROME. THUNDER AND LIGHTNING.
Enter LEON *and* RIFKA.

LEON.—O Rifka, slacken not thy pace as yet;
Exert more strength and make thy limbs obey.
Let's be in haste defying wind and rain,
To find out Jephthah ere it be too late.
Hark! the storm sweeps on with fiendish wrath,
And terror moves throughout the elements;
Loud thunders ride on cloud-veiled cars of fire,
And still Mortara courts this wild tornado,
Without a shelter to protect his silver-head.

RIFKA.—It was unkind of us to leave him so;
We ought t'have stayed in spite of his command.

LEON.—Disobedience teems bright buds of gratitude,
When yielding might endanger who command.
Methinks, dear sister, 't was wrong in us to go;
We should have forced him to return with us.

RIFKA.—He would not stir; I tried to move his will.
His mind is set to speak with Austria ——

LEON.—Who does approach, my sister?

RIFKA.—I can not make them out.

LEON.—I'll gaze.

8*

RIFKA.—List! they're near.
Hide, I prithee hide, my brother.

LEON.—Why, foolish maid, fear makes thee blind ;—
Behold young Jephthah and good Abraham.

Enter JEPHTHAH *and* ABRAHAM.
Well met, my friends.

JEPHTHAH.—Speak, if ye have urgent business.
We are in haste and can not tarry long.
Mortara has been gone from us since morn,
Nor know we what's become of him.

LEON.—Of him I fain would speak.

JEPHTHAH.—Ye saw him, then?

LEON.—We did, friend Jephthah.

RIFKA.—In yon black forest's road, where lofty trees
Expel bright day, and owls wild omens shriek,
He waiteth for the Austrian minister,
To take his brief into the council-room :
Since Pope nor envoy heeded what he said,
But shoved him back when he did sue to them.
He weeps and raves—defies the tempest's rage,
And mocks the thunders shaking this our firmament.
Stalks to and fro—a prey to bitter grief,
Like hoary Priam at brave Hector's fall.

ABRAHAM.—And ye have left him quite alone.

LEON.—As sister said : his purpose is
To meet with Austria.

JEPHTHAH.—Shame! shame upon ye!—shame!
Where was your heart to leave th' old man alone?
Where was your love to melt the stony heart ?
Aye, ingratitude is best of currency,
And disrespect to age a praise in man.
Why! e'en a brute to see him thus exposed,
Though void of reason would have stayed with him,
To guard the life which instinct him directs.

LEON.—Be not too hasty in thy judgment, Jephthah,
Else thou may'st rue the quickness of thy mind.
It grieves me much, to be misunderstood,
For so I am, or wouldst not think me void of pity.
It was his will, that we at once depart,
Nor did he hear us more, although we begged
To be around him, till the whirlwind stops:
Or if he chooses we'd take him to a shelter,
To which he had but one reply:—go, my children—go.
'Twas he who sent us forth—aye, with means,
To seek a home beyond th' Atlantic sea.

RIFKA.—He did desire us to depart at once.

LEON.—He did.

JEPHTHAH.—So soon?—adieu;—
Ne'er cease to walk in virtue's path.
Good Leon, a thousand pardons do I crave,
As my great love for this old man, mine uncle,
Caused me to be ungenerous to my friend.
Forgive the wrong, it wounds me to the core.

RIFKA.—Noble youth.

LEON.—As I do hope, prosperity be mine,
And wish Mortara's son redeemed again:
Thy hand I press in token of my love.

JEPHTHAH.—Let those refuse, who know not friendship's
worth ;
May such as thou make up what I in brothers lack.

ABRAHAM.—We do progress but slowly in our search.

JEPHTHAH.—Since we on earth may never meet again,
For something tells me—'tis not fear—no,—no:
That Jephthah soon be buried with the dead,
Have no ill feelings for the orphan-youth,
Though his rude manners oft offended ye.

LEON.—May'st thou long live in peace and happiness.

RIFKA.—To know thee is to love thee.

ABRAHAM.—Let's on, good Jephthah.
Farewell good friends.

JEPHTHAH.—Here is a hand for both.—Now adieu.

(*Exit* ALL.)

SCENE 4TH.—THE PONTIFF'S COUNCIL-ROOM.

Pius seated on his throne, surrounded by Cardinal Savelli, Bishop Bedini, two prelates, Prussia, France and Bavaria. England kneeling before the chair of State, with Mortara's brief in his hand.

PIUS.—Rise, Montefiore, and drop this useless suit.

(MONTEFIORE arises.)

Though weeping be our heart and deep our woe,
To recollect Mortara's poignant grief,
For having lost the staff of his old age:
Yet more than equal is our sacred love
To virgin Mary and our holy church,
Whose faithful servant we are blessed to be.
As man—we mix our sighs and tears with his;
Contract our brow and robe ourselves in black;
Deliver prayers up to strengthen him—
In short, our sorrow proves no less than his.
But as the Pontiff of our holy God,
Prime minister designed to rule the earth,
And make each nation humble to our faith:
We at its head, complying to His will,
Forget ourself in whom we represent.
All gentle feelings vanish in our rank,
Save those who dignify the force of Rome.
This child must stay with us; no Hebrew he,
But as a Catholic must he grow up.
Mortara lives a second childhood o'er;
His reason failed him—so our court proclaimed.
If this be so, Rome in stern duty bound,
Must rear the boy as he can serve her best.
Church and state are one, and being so,
We claim each man to labor for our cause;

Each soul to worship at the Papal shrine.
Then choke complaints like this ere they escape,
And let us hear no more such grievances.
It ruffles us to see thee here espouse
A cause unworthy of Great Britain's name.

MONTEFIORE.—I urge no more, against your mighty will,
This humane suit which brought me to your court.
My mission spurned, I beg your holy leave,
To sail for England and my sovereign,
Who does defy the power of your Grace.
(*Exit* MONTEFIORE.)

PIUS.—Savelli! Bedini!—Prelates of our church!
Have ye not marked great Britain's minister?
By our Grace! we think he threw the glove at us;
France! canst thou be still to this great insult?—
Savelli! England has been plain with us;——
May all the fiends of hell oppose her reign!
Ha, ha! she does defy our power—
What say'st thou France?—Great Britain's up;
And thou, Bavaria! canst brook the challenge?
Where's thy wonted mettle?—in thy gape?——
Cardinal! our brothers seem amused;
What's that! the Pope is still the Pope of Rome.

PRUSSIA.—If 't be no wrong to differ with your Grace,
Methinks his suit should not have been opposed.

PIUS.—Prussia! Prussia! we know thee well;——
Good—good!—ha, ha, excellent.
What right hast thou to judge the Pontiff's deed?

PRUSSIA.—Since you, most holy sir, demand reply,
And Prussia never fears to speak his mind,
I frankly tell you why I dared to judge,
And why I disapproved——

PIUS.—Disapprove?—Cardinal!——
Good servants of the church you may depart.
(*Exit* PRELATES.)

Cardinal! Prussia disapproves;——
Protestant! speak no more—speak no more.

    PRUSSIA.—I beg your gracious favor to return.

    PIUS.—'T is granted.   (*Exit* PRUSSIA.)

May destruction be thy kingdom's doom;
Be this thy benediction!
Though Italy revolts and England threatens Rome;
Though Prussia dares to disapprove our course——
France!—Cardinal! 's death—France, I say—

    FRANCE.—Your holy Grace.

    PIUS.—Your holy Grace——France!—O, France:
Thou hast outgrown thyself;—'t is good——
Thou art emperor now—who cares who made thee one?
No, no; the world asks not what thou hast been,
But what thou art: and thou art emperor.
France! thou art slow in comprehension;—
Come; thy word, if thou wilt deign and speak.
Dost thou approve of what we've done?

    FRANCE.—England is condemned for the defiance shown,
Yet with your leave, most holy sire, I think
You were too hasty with great Montefiore.
The outrage done by Rome's inquisitors,
Fills' mind and heart with horror and dismay.
He sued for mercy at your gracious hand,
Which, if he meant to quarrel or to chafe,
Could have dispensed with smooth civilities,
And straight demanded what he pleaded for.
France loves the church—reveres her mighty chief; .
Defends her rights, but can't endorse her wrong.
I therefore too will supplicate and beg
Your holy Grace to free this Hebrew boy.

    PIUS.—What! show to earth we fear her censure?
Confess an instability of purpose?
Abandon our crusade and mope in shame?
Suckle liberty and lose our sway?
Never, never; we swear it, never.

FRANCE.—Rome is all powerful.

PIUS.—Thou mockest well;—yet think of Bonaparte,
And tremble at the doom awaiting thee.
Go, conspire with Britain 'gainst our power,
And swell the number of our enemies.
Assist the rebels of th' Italian states;
Apostatize and lead th' insurgents on.
Though Rome deserted by her French ally,
And meanly shifted from Bavaria's prince—
Our cry is still: on, on, inquisitors!
Subdue the world and prove the Pope her chief.
We still have Austria to redress this wrong;
To teach obedience to the Pontiff's will.
By St. Peter! dread Hapsburg is awake.

Enter PEDROLDA.

How now?

PEDROLDA.—Austria sleeps in death, your Grace.
PIUS.—A trick! by our faith, a trick!—Monk——
PEDROLDA.—O, holy sire, in what have I offended?
PIUS.—We'll excommunicate thee from the church, liar.
PEDROLDA.—O, sacred sire, I saw him dead myself.

PIUS.—Begone. (*Exit* PEDROLDA.)

Rome, Rome; this is an evil omen.
The court adjourns indefinitely, my sons.
Depart to your kingdoms with our blessing.
Go, we wave ceremonies at this sorry news.

(Exit FRANCE and BAVARIA.)

An evil omen—an evil omen.
Come Savelli! Bedini!—to my side;—
How do we look? is our forehead blanched?
Our cheek, ashy?—O, we feel oppressed.
Savelli; it was untimely news.
Let us forth.

SAVELLI.—Not yet, great Pius; Cornelia, the sister,
Awaiteth now her trial.

Pius.—Have her brought in at once, good brothers,
Ourself will this day witness her confession.

Savelli.—Whom shall we send to wait on her, great sire,
Pedrolda who commissioned to attend,
Your sentence separated from the church?

Pius.—Reinstate him in his office; invest him
With this holy charge.—It is our mandate.
                    (*Exit* Savelli and Bedini.)
Poor is the policy to war at home,
When all the world gives signs of enmity.
Ten thousaand foes around a castle's walls,
The ramparts scaling with loud musketry,
Can be repulsed and put to shameful flight,
If the besieged in unison charge forth.
But when dissension splits who should agree,
Or one base coward from within betrays:
He singly can destroy and lay in waste,
What Theseus guards and Hercules defends.
To terrify th' insurgent multitude,
And force rebellious nations to submit:
To find us feared abroad—revered in Rome,
Ourself must prove an Ajax in the field—
A Nestor garbed in Numa's sacred gown.
For wisdom must retain what courage gains.
Who's there?
                    (*Enter* Pedrolda and Cornelia.)

Pedrolda.—Your holy servant brings Cornelia.

Cornelia.—Thrice holy sire, in meekness let me kneel.
          (She kneels before Pius and kisses his toe.)

Pius.—Submission to our mandates is a grace,
Which brings salvation and true happiness.
We, in great mercy to redeem mankind
Demand obedience, which if withheld will doom,
The soul to hell and black, eternal death.

CORNELIA.—O, woe is me, of having lost a Heaven;
My soul is grieved at what my heart hath done.
Will godly sorrow and true penitence,
Wipe off the stains of sin and wash us pure?

PIUS.—Rise daughter and confess thy breach of duty;
Thy sighs bespeak a non-compliant will.
What hast thou done with our authority,
Which we were pleased to give unto thy hand,
To serve the church and weaken her great foes?

CORNELIA.—Have mercy on my soul, thrice gracious sire.

PIUS.—Where is the rebel Jephthah?—answer us.

CORNELIA.—Have pity—pity, oh! pity me.

PIUS.—May'st thou be damned for needing pity.
Where's Jephthah.

CORNELIA.—O, let your anger not be spent on me;
I am unworthy of so just a wrath.

PIUS.—To hell and hide thy features, fallen wretch.

CORNELIA.—O, pardon, sire, the virgin's votary,
Who has been guilty of deceptious cheat.

PIUS.—Rise and speak: what hast thou done with Jephthah?

CORNELIA.—I saved him, sire;—have mercy on my soul.

PIUS.—Let loose thy hold; pollution stains thy hands.

CORNELIA.—I'm undefiled, although I saved the youth.
Deny me not your holy benediction.

PIUS.—Draw no nearer to our sacred Majesty;——
Come, ope thy heart and cleanse it to the core.
Speak, what hast thou done with Jephthah?

CORNELIA.—O, gracious sire, allay your rage awhile,
And curse me not while I unfold my heart.
If such a deed can seal mine own perdition,
Consigning future bliss far from my reach:
Then damn me if you will—what matters it?
I would not live to know my Faith so black.

9

I am a woman prone to change and love;
Unruly blood flows in mine arteries;
Each single drop conveys a lustful wish,
And through my system sweeps a secret joy.
The mind expands while heart and pulse beat high,
And tender thoughts awake in strong desire,
Until the muscles hued to tulip red,
Move every bone and fire the nimble limbs.
The eye once dull, throws off her drowsy veil,
And brightens in the ardor love excites.
A mellow flame spreads 'round the sparkling orb,
And luscious mildness laughs through every glance.
The socket swells below the shaded arch,
And winks subdued a studied coyness feign.
The apple weeping tears of happiness,
So softly yielding to voluptuous dreams,
Draws down the curtain to indulge the thrill,
Which for a moment agitates the frame,
And melts the heart with sensual luxury,
Whose balmy sweetness mocks the bliss of heaven,
And grants to earth a favor steeped in milk,
To prick impassioned youth and heat the breast.
So are our feelings ruling—and obeyed.
In vain we stifle nature in its growth.
I sought the convent and the sacred shrine,
And in retirement wished to spend my days,
To prove a virgin and desert the world;
Her ways to shun and seek eternal life.
I daily prayed for strength to keep my vow,
And fit me to the service of our church,
Until at last I thought me strong enough,
To deal with our great foe and punish him.
But O, great sire, when I beheld this youth,
More beautiful than Fancy could have drawn,
Approach me gently, kneeling at my feet,
Enquiring how the holy vestal fares,

In tones far sweeter than the nightingale's :
I doubted whether such as he were base.
At last my scornful looks drove from his lips,
A mild reproof for mine ungentleness.
He took my hand and held it to his breast,
Exclaiming : " sister, spurn no orphan boy."
O, holy sire, 't was then I pitied him,
And loved the heart so lorn and sensitive.
He raised his eyes and tears rolled down his cheeks ;
I met his glance and felt my sex prevail.
In yon inclosure where I bade adieu
To all the scenes I prized, and took the veil,
He often met me in the twilight hour,
To sing and speak of brighter days to me.
At last he wooed me from the sacred shrine,——

PIUS.—And then ?—go on—thou didst consent ?

CORNELIA.—No, gracious sire, I steeled the yielding heart,
And resolute became my faltering speech.
I spurned his offer with emphatic sneers,
To pierce his bosom and to make it bleed.
So he may leave me never more to come,
And shun the spot his presence sacred made.
I spared his life and saved him from your wrath,
And no one suffers by this loss but I.
My mission and your plan in secret sleep ;
The tongue betrayed not though she disobeyed.
Resistless were his manners and his love—
So fearless, yet so modest in his ways,
That gazing, could disarm a Nero's rage,
And strip him bare in spite of his intent.
Thrice gracious Pontiff! I could not harm him.
Curse me if you will.

PIUS.—For this auricular confession, wretch,
Hear thy dread sentence and our royal mind.

CORNELIA.—I am resigned.

Pius.—For disobedience to our stern command,
And for the boldness to deceive our Grace,
We now expel thee from the eucharist
And from the sacred duties of the shrine.
Our curse is thine and may it follow thee
Throughout this life to blast each tender hope.

Cornelia.—Be merciful—oh! be merciful.

Pius.—Kneel, wretch, and further hear thy doom.

Cornelia.—O, gracious sire, I can not suffer more.

Pius.—Like some base culprit will we stripe thy back,
And feed thee on ground glass and spider-wombs,
Until thy skin turns green, and all the flesh
Breeds ulcers to torment thee with the plague.

Cornelia.—O, horror, horror!—how terrible my doom!

Pius.—Then when thy hide screens but the skeleton,
We lash thee from thy cell to dance on pins,
And make thee swallow balls of burning lead,
Till from thy eyeballs shoots a deadly glare,
And on thy features rage convulsive spasms.

Cornelia.—Make me not mad; it is too black a threat.

Pius.—Keep thy damned tongue and hear us out,
Else in our sight we'll have thee minced.

Cornelia.—O, slay me, sire, and spare me from yon doom.

Pius.—Not quite alone shalt suffer for this crime,
Our Grace intends no less a penalty
For Jephthah. Ere the bat obscures the air,
Or steals on sleep to suck the blood of man,
Wilt thou and he be lodged in custody.
Inquisitor! away with her.

Cornelia.—O, spare him, sire; he is too good to suffer.

Pius.—Away with her. Away.

(*Exit* Cornelia and Pedrolda.)

This night will make me master o'er the knave;
His doom is death—but this sweet wench we'll save.

(*Exit* Pius.)

SCENE 5TH.—A ROOM IN MORTARA'S DWELLING.

Mortara surrounded by Abraham and Sir Montefiore; Jephthah loitering in the background.

MONTEFIORE.—Our comfort is in having done our duty;
Discouragement brings ever ill success.
What we essayed is laudable in us.
Our first appeal shall sire as many more,
As we can offer and he dares oppose.
His insolence will irritate the world,
And with one voice she'll thunder at his gates,
And make him tremble ev'n in great Rome.

ABRAHAM.—Thy boy, my friend, will be redeemed again;
He can't withhold what all the world demand.

MORTARA.—And was he deaf to all entreaties?

MONTEFIORE.—Ne'er a tyrant reigned, but would have been
     more yielding.

MORTARA.—O Israel! Israel! what a sufferer art thou!

MONTEFIORE.—Our sun is rising; let's be brave and provi-
     dent.
Few are the countries still oppressing us.
Behold, Great Britain has indorsed our cause;
In all her Peers John Russell's spirit moves.

ABRAHAM.—And free Columbia—a blessing to the land—
Shields many of our wary Sentinels;
Reformer Wise has raised his Clarion voice,
And Senior Leeser heard thy bitter woe.
Like two young lions reeking in their gore,
The bolder wax for being chafed and pricked,
So these brave leaders sally in the fray,
While wounded justice animates their souls,
To save the boy and chastise popery.

MORTARA.—Sweet Hope! live on and cheat me with thy
     smile,
Discern my grave and ghastly glare on it;
I'm weary now and would embrace thee, Death!

9*

There is no need for this old man to live.
My hairs are white like silver spun in threads,
And this long beard resembles clearest snow.
My heart is torn—this brow in sorrow bends;
These fleecy curls now playing with the wind,
With fitting paleness mock the transient world,
Infusing prelibation of a better state.

MONTEFIORE.—O, hoary sage, lose not your fortitude.

MORTARA.—Aye, Montefiore, it was my son—my Yulah's
boy.
I am resigned—but tears will trickle down the cheeks.

ABRAHAM.—My dearest friend, affliction bows thee low;
Pray, bear it meekly—God, will end it soon.

MORTARA.—Bear it meekly? Aye, I do not murmur.
Abraham, I am foolish—an old, doting fool.
Let me lament my loss—I ask no more.
Is it strange? why! am I not a father?

ABRAHAM.—A virtuous son is thine——

MORTARA.—Is?—was; good Abraham! Where is he now?
In some dismal dungeon taught to hate his sire.

ABRAHAM.—This absence will increase his love, dear friend.
And in due time he will return to thee,
To bless thy years and guard thy mellow age.

MORTARA.—Where will I be then?—In my grave.

ABRAHAM.—Why, many happy hours hast yet to live;
The monster must relent and Benjamin returns.

MORTARA.—Never, never! he is chained and I must die.
Montefiore! where art thou, Montefiore?—here?
Come, tell me, Montefiore: is Pius old as I?
Is he—no, no; he would not slay a child.
Montefiore! Montefiore! my mind is wandering——
I can't control my heart;—Montefiore!

MONTEFIORE.—Mortara——

MORTARA.—Help me to yon seat;—here let me muse awhile.

MONTEFIORE.—Now tranquilize your mind in gentle sleep:
My ill success over-wrought his brain.

ABRAHAM.—A slumber would invigorate him;
Look! he sleeps not, but all the thoughts
That so commoved him, pass through a reverie.

MONTEFIORE.—Pray let's aside: our gaze may discompose
him.

JEPHTHAH, (in front.)—At last the cup is foaming to the
brim;
To add one drop would burst the ulcered heart,
And spread like wild-fire through my very blood.
Too long I watched supinely for redress,
And like a coward shunned an enterprise,
The time demands and fate long since decreed.
Here sits an old—the kindest of old men:
A prey to grief—to bitter agony;
He is mine uncle; aye, my more than sire,
Who nursed this sapling strong and powerful.
Shall I now shrink to spend my little might,
And like a niggard-wretch, fear to perform
A deed prolific of so great a consequence?
By Jehovah! no!—I will redress the wrong!
Why should I crave such life and know and see;
A man I'll die, Mortara's son to free.

ABRAHAM.—Behold young Jephthah brooding o'er some grief.

JEPHTHAH.—Strong motives now to stronger acts incite;
Each moment teems reproaches for my tardiness.
Mortara weeps—who should remove the cause
Save I, that owes him most, yet offers least?
I am unloved; my death shall prove no loss;
Few tears will flow should dangers cut me off.
I fill no heart to make me cling to earth,
Where I unclaimed intrude 'round foreign hearths.

MONTEFIORE.—Has he some private sorrow on his mind?

ABRAHAM.—None, to my knowledge, but what we in common
feel.

JEPHTHAH —To be not loved, and those I cherished are no
    more ;
What else can now entice me to stay idle,
While I can serve this man, who still remains
Conspicuous in his grief my counterpart ?

MONTEFIORE.—Deep emotions seem to sway his heart.

JEPHTHAH.—Why like some craving knave hold fast to life,
Which but to risk would terminate in gain.
Dread are my means—a firm and mighty will ;
Rage swells my veins and death falls from mine arm ;
The mind is fixed ; great Pius lives no more——
He or I shall seek the styxian shore.   (He retires a little.)

ABRAHAM.—Methinks Mortara bade thee to approach.

MORTARA.—Sir Montefiore, art thou for England soon ?

MONTEFIORE.—The morrow's sun shines not on me in Rome.

MORTARA.—Tell not my people on Great Britain's isle,
The weakness I have shown at thy success.
It took me by surprise, and being old
The heart ran o'er ;—but now I'm nerved again.

MONTEFIORE.—We all are men ; to feel insures a soul.
Behold your nephew comes.

MORTARA.—Where is my Jephthah ?—where ?

JEPHTHAH.—Here at your feet; what would mine uncle have?

MORTARA.—Thy love, my son.

JEPHTHAH.—Bless me, uncle.

MORTARA.—May Jehovah guard thee from temptation,
And plant thee in His favor and His love,
That thou may'st prosper while thou livest.

ALL.—Amen.

MORTARA.—Now rise, my son; embrace thy loving uncle.
JEPHTHAH.—Do you love me, uncle ?
MORTARA.—Almost as well as Benjamin ;—he was my boy.
JEPHTHAH.—But still not quite as well.

Mortara.—I love thee, Jephthah, with a father's love.
Art thou not all to me now?

Jephthah.—Now?—pardon, uncle—pardon me.

Mortara.—Rise; come let me behold thy countenance.
(Jephthah rises.)

Jephthah.—Strong is mine arm, good uncle.

Mortara.—O, ever wield it in a noble cause.

Jephthah.—I will, mine uncle.—Now my word is pledged.
I go to prove it in the Pontiff's death.

Mortara.—Thou shalt not murmur—vengeance is mine
own:
So speaks Jehovah;—hear it, Jephthah, hear.

Jephthah.—Shall we forever wear the Roman chain,
And lick the foot which kicks us wantonly?
No; damned Pius dead and we are free.
His thousand prelates like so many slaves,
Move by his will and see but through his eyes.
His voice but hushed—his gaze once closed in death,
Their hate grows harmless as an untoothed cur's.

Abraham.—Believe it not that they are void of sting;
Through every priest peeps out a little Pope.

Mortara.—When Providence decrees to end our woes,
Without a deed of wrong he'll set us right.
Then, pray, desist from this foul purpose, son,
And stain thy brow not with so black a crime.
Be thou to me what Benjamin has been,
And wean my heart to thy affections, youth.

Jephthah.—Wean it, uncle?—aye, I will wean it.
What shall I do?—remind you of times past?
How you did fondle Benjamin?

Mortara.—I prithee, Jephthah, sing his love to me.

Jephthah.—Uncle, will it make you very happy?

Mortara.—Speak but of him—but of my gentle boy,

And all the world I shall forget at once,
And see and hear but Benjamin.

JEPHTHAH.—Forget all the world?—weep, orphan weep.
Uncle, I will do my best to make you happy?

MORTARA.—I know thou wilt;—embrace me in its truth.

JEPHTHAH.—Here, uncle, the orphan gives his pledge.

MORTARA.—God bless thee, youth.

ALL.—Amen.

JEPHTHAH.—Thanks, gentlemen, thanks.
The orphan weeps to be so needy of a blessing.

MORTARA.—O, gracious Heaven, let me forget all woe,
And let thy blessings on my Jephthah flow!
I soon will die—advance him in Thy Grace;
Be thou his parent to direct his ways.

Enter JUDAH.

What brings thee trembling in my sight?
Speak Judah!

JUDAH.—Rome's inquisitors are below; there's danger nigh.
Hear——

LUDOVICO, (without.)—Is this Mortara's room?

(Without.)—It is.

Enter LUDOVICO.

LUDOVICO.—A fair day, gentlemen.

MORTARA.—What would the inquisitor of Mortara?

LUDOVICO.—I am in quest of Jephthah, not of thee,
Let him appear; I must have speech with him.

JEPHTHAH.—Here I am; what wants the Pope of me?

LUDOVICO.—His holy Grace would hear thine own defense,
To a grave charge thou stand'st accused of.
His warrant am I bid to execute,
Empowering me to levy on thy body straight;
To hold thee in the inquisition-jail,
Till on thy trial thou art guiltless found,

Of stealing into the sacred nunnery,
And hold communion with a virgin there,
To desecrate her life with impure love,
And raise sedition in a peaceful mind.

JEPHTHAH.—Inquisitor! pray, tell me if thou canst,
Who charged me with this crime?

LUDOVICO.—A holy nun; Cornelia is her name.

JEPHTHAH.—Cornelia, my accuser?—Why 'tis well;
Inquisitor! will she be at my trial?

LUDOVICO.—'Tis very probable.
But come; keep thy queries for another time.

JEPHTHAH.—Lead on, I follow but my destiny.

MORTARA.—Hold! Mortara bids ye, hold.
Art thou mad to seek destruction—even death?

JEPHTHAH.—Uncle, deny me not so sweet a fate,
As dying when Cornelia bids me to;
I wooed her love and saw her smile on me;
It costs my life, but's worth a thousand such.
Then give me leave to face the treacherous dame,
And drink the bitter cup she filled for me.

MORTARA.—Nay, my son, Mortara bids thee stay.
I am too old to do without thee now,
And thou too young to cope with priestly wile.
No crime does stain thy brow; so go not hence;
Or wilt thou leave me to mourn another son?
I would sink in the grave a heart-broken man;
The cold earth as my bed, and thou the cause.
I can not outlive it.—O, Jephthah stay.

JEPHTHAH.—I'm yours, mine uncle, yours.—Behold, I stay.

MORTARA.—Kindest, dearest, best of youths.
Inquisitor avaunt! he'll tarry here.
Think'st thou I'll trust him in thy ruthless hands?
Thou! who keepst my Benjamin inthralled?
Thou, who causedst my Yulah's death?

Wouldst thou now take my Jephthah too?
Inquisitor! he stays.

LUDOVICO.—Thwart not my purpose in arresting him;
It is my mission and ye must comply.

MORTARA.—Back! insulted age cries back!
Touch him if thou darest and this weak arm,
Shriveled as it is, shall strike thee dead.

JEPHTHAH.—Uncle, retire; I'll manage him myself.

MORTARA.—Go, tell his Grace, Mortara frustrated thee.
Tell him, this hoary head can see his web.
Tell him, he may oppress me—aye, kill me,
But Jephthah shall escape his bitter wrath.

JEPHTHAH.—Uncle — inquisitor ——

LUDOVICO.—Compel me not to injure thy damned head,
Which I shall do if thou dost interfere.

MORTARA.—Strike, if thou wilt.—Assassin, strike!
Here is my breast; where is thy sword to cleave it?
Thou showest no mercy, but to torture more;
Dispatch me quick, and cease to wring my heart.
What! give up my Jephthah too? my wrinkled form,
Though sapless as harsh autumn's withering leaves,
Shall moulder into dust ere I consent.
Would they take thee from me too, my Jephthah?
Tell his sapient Grace, one child he stole of me.
'Tis quite enough.   I thought him far more just,
Else should I've kept my Benjamin from thee,
As I do him.—O, my Jephthah!—avaunt!
They would slay thee,——Yulah, thou art happy; —
Inquisitor! thou heardst mine answer — go.

LUDOVICO.—I will, brave heretic; henceforth beware,
For hindering me in making this arrest.
His holy Grace shall know of what transpired,
And be assured thy maw must soon digest
A mess prepared, which thou wilt not eschew.

(*Exit* LUDOVICO.)

Mortara.—Fly, Jephthah, while thou canst; he'll soon re-
turn,
With force superior to imprison thee.
To England haste with noble Montefiore;
Thou art not safe one hour in Italy.

Jephthah.—Pray, uncle, let me boldly front my judge,
I can defend me from the charges brought.
'Tis true I sought a sister's presence oft,
'Twas after she did bait me with sly winks;
And used such winning means to gain me o'er.
I used no art to woo her from her vow,
Nor did I tempt her ere she tempted me.
This very maid stands my accuser now.

Mortara.—There are inquisitors of every sex;
This nun is one, else would have stayed within,
Hid from thy gaze, as thou, my son, from her's.
Then fly, I do exhort thee, fly at once.
'Twas but a plea to get thee in their net.

Jephthah.—Uncle, I'm mad;—do with me what you will.
Cornelia, so base?—virtue is but mockery;—
Be it as it may, I'll stay with you.
If I must die, fate will pursue me still—
Death is death, come it how it will.

Mortara.—Jephthah!

Jephthah.—Uncle, what would you have of me?

Mortara.—Let me not plead in vain, but get thee gone.
Rome's full of spies; escape in time, I pray.
O, my Jephthah, why dost torture me?

Jephthah.—Our cause is one; I'll live and die with you.

Mortara.—O, fly, my son, soon canst return again.
They'll harm not me, I am not worth their while.

Jephthah.—I'll separate not from you, 'though you bid;
Where'er you stay let Jephthah be your guard.
If I must die, I die as 'tis decreed.
Who can suspend the arm of fate?—not I.

Mortara.—I follow thee to England—ask no more.

Now fly, my son—fly from the Pontiff's wrath.
Mortara begs—commands thee fly.

JEPHTHAH.—Command?—behold, you are obeyed.
I go for your sake—no, not for mine.
Judah! if thou dost love me brotherly,
Guard mine uncle with thy very life;
Heed it, for my sake—thy sake—his sake.

JUDAH.—I swear it.

JEPHTHAH.—'Tis well. We'll meet again—perhaps.
Uncle! bless me ere I go;—now farewell.

MORTARA.—O, my Jephthah;—God be with thee.

JEPHTHAH.—I hope so.
Sir Montefiore! I'll meet you on the French frontier.

MONTEFIORE.—To-morrow I'll depart.

JEPHTHAH.—'T is well.—Adieu—uncle adieu.

MORTARA.—Adieu——

(*Exit* JEPHTHAH.)

For ever.—Friends and thou, great Montefiore,
Pray, guard my Jephthah out of Rome.

(*Exit* ABRAHAM, JUDAH and MONTEFIORE.)

Now is the time to shed the limpid tear,
When all the passions, like a well-spent storm,
Exhausted swoon into a gentle calm.
Now let me take a retrospective view,
While solitude serenely wooes thy mind,
And banished care perturbs not where it grieves.
O, heart! cease throbbing after distant joy,
And throttle sighs obsequious to complaint.
What if the sky be dark—there's providence
In every cloudlet's move;—why then despair?
Mysterious are His ways;—to be content
Man dares not think, else thinking broods revolt.

(*Enter* LUDOVICO with six inquisitors.)

How now?

LUDOVICO.—We come to ask once more for Jephthah,
Whom we'll arrest in Pius' holy name.

Where is he?

MORTARA.—Seek him, inquisitors.

LUDOVICO.—Where is he hid? speak quick and let us know.
By the holy mass! we'll not be crossed again.
Where is he?

MORTARA.—Seek him.

LUDOVICO.—If thou dost keep it from us, here I swear,
Thee to imprison and to torture much,
Until thou wilt cry out his hiding place.

MORTARA.—Take me if thou wilt; I can't but die.

LUDOVICO.—Cursed heretic, be warned and tell us quickly;
Where is the youth?

MORTARA.—Seek him!

LUDOVICO.—Brothers! to the inquisition with him.
Take hold of him——

MORTARA.—Away!—There's not a hound but knows his
  place.
Know yours.
The body's yours—the soul is free as air;
The joy I miss below in Heaven I'll share.
Let me pass.

     (*Exit* MORTARA.)

LUDOVICO.—Inquisitors! follow him.

    (*Exit* LUDOVICO and INQUISITORS.)
     [*End of 3d Act.*]

———

ACT FOURTH.
SCENE 1ST.— THE INQUISITION.
Enter TWO JAILORS.

1ST JAILOR.—Has he been quiet to-night?

2D JAILOR.—Up to this hour I heard him groan—then pray,
So sweetly mournful—so pathetic sweet,
That I, almost to pity moved, sought out yon spot,
To weep when he prayed, and pray when he wept.
Hush!

(MORTARA uttering some low, mournful sounds, within.)

Such wailful sounds escape him constantly.

    1st Jailor.—He brought this bitter fate on him. He is
So stubborn and determinately mute,
That all the terrors of the inquisition,
Can wring not from his heart what she would know.
Hark!

            (Mortara moaning, within.)
It is in sooth a drear and dismal moan.

    2d Jailor.—It is.
Will he not tell where Jephthah refuge sought?

    1st Jailor.—He is as silent as these walls.
Hark! he moans again!

        (Mortara within, cries with excruciating pain.)
He'll soon break down.

    2d Jailor.—I hope he may.—'Twere better for us all.

    1st Jailor.—He will reveal the secret to the grave.

    2d Jailor.—I think as thou; such men will never yield.
But ho!—who comes?

    Pedrolda, (without.)—A man with a cross.

    2d Jailor.—Whither away so late?

    Pedrolda, (without.)—To trail the fox.

    2d Jailor.—The pass is clear ——

        (*Enter* Pedrolda with a lantern.)

    Pedrolda.—To the man of the cross.

    2d Jailor.—Pedrolda?

    Pedrolda.—The same.—How wanes the night?

    2d Jailor.—With no unusual news, save frequent moans,
Which from Mortara's cell came sailing forth.
They were so touching ——

    Pedrolda.—Enough!—What of Cornelia canst report?

    2d Jailor.—She raves no longer.

    Pedrolda.—'Tis well;—now seek thy mat—but stop!
Where is thy partner in patrol?

    1st Jailor.—I'm here, and came in time to his relief.

    Pedrolda.—Now go.— Watch'st thou till morn?

    1st Jailor.—Ludovico so commissioned me.

PEDROLDA.—'T is well.—Now if Cornelia raves again,
Clothe her in the iron blouse.

    1ST JAILOR.—I will.   (*Exit* PEDROLDA.)

Could I but leave this horrid place again,
From whence no mortal man has e'er returned,
Unless a corpse to fill the reeking pit:
Upon my life, not for the Papal crown,
Would I again become a hireling here.
I was too hasty—now it is too late,
Then let me watch—'t is better than to die.
What ho!—who comes?

    LUDOVICO, (without.)—A man with a cross.

    1ST JAILOR.—Whither away so late?

    LUDOVICO, (without.)—To trail the fox.

    1ST JAILOR.—The pass is clear——

(*Enter* LUDOVICO *with* JUDAH *disguised in a black friar's habiliment.*)

    LUDOVICO.—To the man of the cross.

    1ST JAILOR.—Who art thou?

    LUDOVICO.—Ludovico, thy chief!—Good father, halt?

    JUDAH.—Is it much further to Mortara's cell?

    LUDOVICO.—Look! this cross-barred portal leads to him.

    JUDAH.—And has he lodged in here since first he came?

    LUDOVICO.—Ev'n here, for twice twelve months.

    JUDAH.—Good brother! pray, how bears he his confinement?

    LUDOVICO.—Since I have told thee, as we came along,
Why old Mortara was encaved: the rest
Ere we proceed I also will disclose.

    JUDAH.—Much thanks.

    LUDOVICO.—Now hear me, father of St. Lutzen:
When first he was imprisoned in this haunt,
With threats of death dread Pius meant to gain,
Such information he withheld from me.

    JUDAH.—Disclosed he then whence Jephthah fled unknown?

    LUDOVICO.—Pray, hear me out; the sequel will explain.
As fearless as the Macedonian prince,
   10*

Who laughing straddled wild Bucephalus:
And no less calm than martyred Socrates,
Who drank the poison with a steady nerve,
So he received the menace of his Grace,
Without a tremor to denote pale fear.
Then since he brooked such notice undismayed,
His death would still have kept us ignorant.
To gain the end desired we then contrived,
Such measures as we thought would ope his mouth.
With irons sparkling from the furnace' jaw
He suffered us to burn his eyeballs out,
In preference to giving knowledge of the youth.

    JUDAH.—Wretch! and could ye——

      LUDOVICO.—Could we?—Aye, most holy father;
We did refrain our temper from its speed,
And were content with this poor sacrifice.
I know thou think'st us lenient to the knave;
But list: 'twas to increase his punishment.

    JUDAH.—So prudent?
Ye are most circumspect in all your plans.
Pray, tell me what did follow next in suit
To thaw Mortara's pertinacity?

      LUDOVICO.—Too numerous are the tortures we employed,
Here to unfold and thou to listen to;
Yet, holy father will I stop not short,
As long as my narration tires thee not.
Upon a grate placed o'er the smoking coals,
We doomed the white-haired man to roast awhile—
How he did writhe imploring speedy death,
Distorting features in wild agony——
How his blue veins hid in the ashy skin,
Like streams surcharged in raging currents shot
The boiling blood all o'er the roasting frame.
How he then wept still sobbing prayers forth,
While from his fingers' ends dropped off the nails,
From heat in fume ascending through the spit.

Why! Job himself compared to this cursed Jew,
A Hotspur seems in patience to endure.

JUDAH.—Could his frail form sustain such misery?

LUDOVICO.—Like our physicians oft seek antidotes,
Which half-way cure the patient in their care,
To plunge him deeper in disease than erst—
Long keep him so to swell their bill of charge
For forced attendance and prescriptions shown—
Yet wisely hold the sickness in their pale,
That death can't take the sufferer and their pay:
So we to gain the object by dread pangs,
Know well how far to go and when to stop.

JUDAH.—Ye are the keenest of inquisitors.

LUDOVICO.—No sooner saw we that his life would fail,
Than we released him from the fiery grate,
Anointing straight his limbs with liniments,
With juice of herbs to heal and strengthen them.
As some dull ass who bears the marks of blows
More stubborn grows for what he felt and feels—
So this cursed Jew waxed firmer in his pains,
And pangs which make a common mortal shrink,
Raised in his mind a wave of fortitude,
To drown each fear or any weakness found,
And oak-like braved the whirl-wind 'round him raised,
To stand erect, or fall—if fall he must,—
An oak in spite of hell and hellish force.
Yet we at our ill chance were not cast down
To quit the game as long as we had stakes.
Since he persisted in the course he took,
We on the rack then stretched his body out,
In hope that dislocated joints and bones
Might move his adamantean will and loose
The tongue to speak what fear and awe betrays.
But even then he would not yield one jot.

JUDAH.—Noble, noble, O! more than noble.

LUDOVICO.—Pray, praise us not so highly for our deeds,

Else must I think thee not acquainted with
The office of our celibatic race.
Aye, holy father, hadst thou with me been here,
When yon vile wretch, upon death's engine lay—
Thy heart would have rejoiced.—I know it would.

    JUDAH.—I do not doubt it.

    LUDOVICO.—And yet, while he did suffer on the rack,
Confessions none could we extort from him.
Although we gradually stretched limb from limb,
Until his skeleton-form appeared to burst,
And every bone seemed snapping from its mate.
His face which was long since of sickly green,
Grew pale as death—his eyes waxed black as hell,
While from his lips—as blue as frozen gore—
His teeth extended in wild agony.
How they then clattered shooting from the gum
To bite the anguish of the soul in twain.
Why! father, though the rack was used in vain,
It was a worthy prelude to our work.

    JUDAH.—Too mild an introduction to such sport.

    LUDOVICO.—Aye, hardly was his frame restored in strength,
Then we once more resumed the task begun:
Stripped bare, we did besmear with honey sweet,
The naked body then exposed to wasps
To draw his blood, to bite and blister him.
With hands and feet in fetters tightly bound,
His form within a basket was swung up,
To swarms of horn-mouthed insects to succumb.
It was a sight—Oh! what a horrid sight!
On every pore the greedy sucklers hung,
Like one huge cloud of blackness, covering thick
The bleeding body with a file of stings.
The blood came oozing freely from the heart,
And yet his eyes were calm—so quietly fixed,
That we much feared it be the gaze of death—
So steady—still—as if he suffered naught.

JUDAH.—He does possess a god-like fortitude.

LUDOVICO.—Why, by our faith! he did out-zeno-Zeno.
For hear, good father: after all these pangs
He was as contumacious as before.
His holy Grace was ruffled at the knave,
And ordered us to flay his hands and arms.

JUDAH.—What! flay him alive?

LUDOVICO.—Aye, alive;—But what ails thee, father?
Thou tremblest even as an aspen leaf.
What is it that does now perturb thy soul?

JUDAH.—Nothing—nothing;
Hist!

(MORTARA wailing within.)

Whence rose this mournful sound?

LUDOVICO.—From old Mortara's lacerated breast.

JUDAH.—I prithee let me know his latest torture,
The dire effect of which speaks through his moans
A book of penal anguish to the winds.

LUDOVICO.—The interim from the period of the rack,
Down to the youngest of his woes I'll skip,
And by thy holy leave string up my speech,
Now with the causer of that dreary moan.

JUDAH.—Mine ear is thine, good monk.

LUDOVICO.—Since pangs of short duration, oft employed,
Refused the harvest of a single word,
To show us in the welkin of surmise
A shining lamp as beacon to our search,
His holy Grace, the Pontiff of our church
A method of continual suffering planned.
'Tis now a moon since we his scanty meals
First tinctured with ingredients to produce
A painful drought to parch his fauces dry,
And leave him wretched for the want of drink,
Forever craving but a kindly drop.
But as he would have died by thirst provoked,
Unless an antidote were granted him,

We in this drug distilled a precious oil,
Which moistens lungs and keeps the marrow wet,
Yet leaves him yearning with a throat inflamed,
Without the danger of a speedy death,
To end his woes ere we possess the youth.

JUDAH.—Did it produce the much desired effect?

LUDOVICO.—A lily growing on a thistle-plant—
A cedar pregnant with a melon-head—
A sparrow fright'ning eagles in their flight—
A wolf retreating at a lamb's approach—
Fair snow descending on an August-day—
Or showers falling from a cloudless sky:
Had not confounded faculties as much,
And made our eyes in consternation gaze,
As to behold Mortara in distress;
His throat as dry as hay exposed to heat,
Without the plaints attending grief like his.

JUDAH.—Marvelous!—marvelous indeed!

LUDOVICO.—Twice has the earth diurnally revolved,
Since he gives signs of pain from want of drink.
He moans and weeps—implores and prays to God—
As dumb as erst—he won't betray his trust.

JUDAH.—No living soul had ever had such patience.

LUDOVICO.—The gloomy clouds which spread all o'er the
    sky,
And fell in torrents from the upper realm,
To deluge earth and leave no rack behind—
Though filled with oceans spent at last their strength.
So Pius, pattern of great fortitude,
Too long with patience hoping for success,
At last determined now to end this play,
By slaying this old knave or hear him speak.

JUDAH.—When will his execution take place?

LUDOVICO.—If he recants not ere the western hills
Turn rosy with the sun emerging now,
The pale-faced moon will guide his soul to hell.

JUDAH.—And will his holy grace be witness to his death ?

LUDOVICO.—His sacred presence will be necessary
To well interrogate the dying wretch.
A single word—should one escape his lips,
May teem with complication of some friend,
Who, fearing Pius, can be worked upon,
To ravel out the network of this weaver.

JUDAH.—The holy Pontiff!
Will he traverse the street of Rome at night,
Where every man will wondering stare at him,
And follow him—why, even to these doors ?

LUDOVICO.—No, holy friend, completer are our ways.
A subterranean passage from his chamber
Leads straight to this our inquisition-vault.

JUDAH.—And knows Mortara that he must die to-night ?

LUDOVICO.—Not yet, good friend.
But come ; the east is bathing in a blush.
I now will take thee to his christianed son,
Ere yonder bell strikes forth the hour of mass.
Come.   (*Exit* LUDOVICO, JUDAH and JAILOR.)

SCENE 2D.— A STREET IN ROME.
Enter JEPHTHAH and LEON.

JEPHTHAH.—Once more in Rome.
Be praised, Jehovah ! for the favor shown,
During our absence from our native shore,
Whence we with bold determination steered,
To fall a prey to the inquisitors,
Or from their grasp release my suffering kin.
Uncle, uncle, why did I leave you here?
Why did I not foresee this black event?

LEON.—O, dearest friend, cease mourning for a while,
And let us act in concert with our will.
Let's seek brave Judah in his friar-garb,
And gain such information he can give,
Since his last letter bade us haste to Rome.

JEPHTHAH.—Rome! great and time-honored Rome!
Sweet are the memories connected with thy name,
Still dear to my soul although her bitter foe.
Here, aye, even here mine infant-years were spent,
And not a nook throughout thy breadth and length,
But heard the laughter of my childish glee.
How happy was I then!—a little boy; —
Why! a mere child unconscious of its doom.
Aye, then the world appeared a place of joy,
For little children to be playing in.
To see the sun chase off the silver moon,
As he does tinge the sky with laughing fire!
And note the sleeping rose hid in her bud
Crowned with the gentle dew, awake at day,
As golden rays kiss off the crystal tears,
That she may greet the morn with blushing charms.
To think all day, how happy man must be,
When even children find this life so sweet.
O, venerable father!—shade of my mother!
Look down upon your orphan boy, and see,
The change stern fate wrought on his brow.—
Dost know me yet, my mother?—I'm alone!
  LEON.—Pray, Jephthah, be more man.
Take consolation in the thought—
  JEPHTHAH.—Take consolation!—Friend, thou mockest me.
Consolation! —
Why! give it to some wretch, but not to me.
Look thou! beneath this earth sleeps now my sire —
My mother, brothers, sisters—all are dead.
They loved me well, and I—O! how I loved!
But now that holy passion born within the soul—
Forsaken and deserted burns in vain.
Like a dull light seen flickering in some cell,
Far gloomier makes the dungeon with its flame:
So weeping love, neglected by the world,
Broods murkier melancholy o'er the mind,

Than had it never entered in the breast.
I prithee, friend, throw milky words away,
And let my sulky nature woo despair,
And murmur curses on my natal day.
For who can cure disease not understood?
Why, nine times out of ten, the antidote,
Which should allay the pain increases it.
Give me therefore the man who like myself
Without an aim stalks through earth's masquerade—
Alone!—how dreary sounds that word—alone!
No one to claim him,—but like a frail bark
Is thrown from wave to wave until she sinks.
Aye, bring me face to face with such a man,
That I may clasp his hands most brotherly,
And weep upon his breast a sea of tears.
For he alone can sympathize with me,
Who feels the very thorns that sting my soul.
But come; I know thou lovest me from the core,
But show thy friendship not by pitying me.
Now to the point; let's straight to Judah go;
Mortara suffers more than we do know.
Mine uncle will we rescue—what say'st thou?
Unsheathe thy sword!—let Heaven hear our vow!
(*Exit* JEPHTHAH and LEON.)

SCENE 3D.—A DUNGEON IN THE INQUISITION.
Mortara seated on a mat; blind; his hands and arms flayed. His bosom is exposed, still bleeding.

MORTARA.—Now is the laughing hour of morn, when mists arise,
Dissolving in the smiles of new-born day;
And nature radiant in her blushing garb
Awakes her songsters to salute the sun.
Now choral music rides on every breeze,
And happy sympathy invites our ear.
Each lawn and woodland like Aeolian harps
11

Kissed by the wind send forth sweet melodies.
The lusty fledgling with unfeathered wings
Leaps from the nest and joins the marshaled choir,
And euphemistic grows the dulcet strain.
Now man—earth's lord—forsakes his couch of rest,
And sallies forth as some endangered slave,
To flee from fate and stem the tide of time.
O fool! O fool! what fool art thou, O man!
The very mind which should have made thee king,
And crowned thee monarch of this breathing realm,
Once more aroused, renewed from balmy sleep
Does use the strength acquired to banish peace.
The spotted tookay creeping in the dust,
The clumsy toad with thick and warty skin,
The viviparous bat upon the Ternate-isle,
The small-eyed mole in plowing through the ground,
The shrill-voiced cricket chirping in the hearth,
The buzzard flying with the wings of death,
O man! outstrip thee far in happiness,
And are more blessed in being what they are,
Than thou with thoughts to learn thy littleness.
O, shame! O, shame! to claim a soul divine,
And have less mercy than the fiercest brute.
Even the stately lioness
Whose want of god-like reason is supplied
By instinct, which does raise her 'bove mankind,
Shows far more pity by devouring him,
Who fain would rob her of her suckling whelps
Than thou, O being, with a heart to love,
Forever studying tortures with that heart.
What are my crimes that thou shouldst treat me thus?
What have I done deserving worse than death?
Mine orbless sockets cry out, shame, O shame!
My bleeding breast is witness to thy sins!
My broken limbs have felt thy cruelties!
Mine arms who were for three score years and ten.

Obedient to the impulse of a soul,
Were never raised to wrong the vilest slave;
O, horror! horror! have been flayed by thee,
And crieth unto God for vengeance deep.
All's darkness here, I have no eyes to gaze;
Day has no light for me; my vision's gone.
The sun emerging from the hazy east,
No longer glads the heart of this old man.
His rays invite strange spectres from their haunts,
To flit across my mind in phantom form.
Methinks I see myself,—O, get thee gone!
Avaunt! and show me not—Oh! show me not
This wan and haggard face!—Avaunt, avaunt!
Starvation sits upon thy ridgy brow,
And death is grinning through thy hollow cheeks!
Look! blood in streams runs from his breast, and Oh!
These hands and arms—no, no! they are not mine!
They can not be the silver-headed man's.
And yet I do remember well the rack,
The wasps and all those tortures of mine age,
Which with mine inward eye calls up the past.
          Enter 1st JAILOR with a bowl of soup.
Weep not my soul, and thou, O heart be still!
Let not these tortures mar thy life as well
As form. Threescore and ten with trembling voice
Speak through this parched throat but few words more,
And then, ah then, earth will have done with me.
No trials more for this weak, helpless man;
No tears to flow—no rack to break his limbs;
No, no! no rack.
    1st JAILOR.—Prisoner.
    MORTARA.—Who calls?
    1st JAILOR.—'T is I, thy Jailor.—Here's food for thee.
    MORTARA.—How high is now the sun?
    1st JAILOR.—Some two hours high methinks, although the
      clouds

Are thick this morn and keep the sun locked up.

MORTARA.—Think'st thou t'will rain to-day?

1ST JAILOR.—The atmosphere is thick and sultry, sir,
And heaven indicateth heavy rain.

MORTARA.—When spirits leave their tenements of clay,
To seek the shore of everlasting bliss,
'Tis said, earth falls into a murky gloom,
And showers drench her face in million tears.
O, had I but a drop of all these tears,
To cool my throat and quench the gnawing thirst,
I'd barter for it jewels dear and rare—
The blessings of a silver-headed man.

1ST JAILOR.—I prithee, sir, drink now this bowl of broth,
Thy scanty meal for four and twenty hours.
Upon this wooden bench I sat it down,
As I'm forbid to reach it in thy hands.

MORTARA.—The socket's empty where the eye once rolled,
And all external objects are as night.
The limbs once nimble are too stiff to move
In search of what I can no longer see.
My hands and arms—Oh! look at them—pray look!
Can't even hold the bowl I now must seek.
O, what a fate to be in need of sight,
To look at things to which he'd close his eyes;
To crave strong limbs obedient to the will,
When exercise alone is for the free.
To wail for arms which were they sound and quick,
By every stir would pierce the wounded hand.
O, O, 'tis very foul!

(He walks toward the bench.)

Where am I now!

1ST JAILOR.—In the centre of the cell, good sir,
Turn to the right and you will find the bowl.

MORTARA.—I thank thee, Christian,
Thou hast at least some pity for this man.

1ST JAILOR.—With acts I'd prove it, sir, were I at liberty.

MORTARA.—I doubt it not;—I doubt it not.
O, may Jehovah bless thy truly Christian heart.

1st JAILOR.—Amen.

MORTARA.—I can not reach the spot.—I am too weak.

(He sinks down.)

1st JAILOR.—A heart of stone would melt at such a sight.
Come, old man, I'll help thee to yon bench.

MORTARA.—O, Heaven!

1st JAILOR.—Come, good sir——

MORTARA.—O, keep aback! is't not enough for me
To suffer?   (OFFICER retires a pace.)
Wouldst have thy fate as mine?—take care—take care!
A thousand thorns lodge in mine ulcered flesh;
O, how they sting me to the very heart.
My blood is cold—a chill creeps o'er my frame,
And my last breath escapeth even now.

1st JAILOR.—I can't stand still and see thee suffer so.
Had I to die, I'd reach this broth to thee.
We all are men—the Jew and Christian—all.
Why should such hate exist, I know it not.
Here, good man, drink from this seasoned broth,
It will resuscitate thee into life.

MORTARA.—Where is the bowl? Pray, place it in my hands.

1st JAILOR.—Here to thy lips I'll hold it;—drink, good sir.

(MORTARA drinks.)

Now let me put the bowl aside and help thee up.

MORTARA.—Nay, Christian, soon will I be strong enough
To rise. This soup afresh has fed my life.
Again the pulse is calm and regular,
And through my veins the blood does freely flow.

(The JAILOR draws back.)

O man, O man! no mightier than the worm,
Behold Mortara now and know thyself!
A creature of a moment's breath—no more;
To-day—an oak with sweeping boughs to shade
The tall and slender grass around him spread;

11*

To-morrow—shattered, broken by the wind,
Dashed to the ground to rot and be no more.
Thou dost not live; the moment of thy birth
Thou even begin'st to die.—Prepare thyself.

(MORTARA rises and moves toward his mat.)

How many pass away from this dull earth,
Who'd fondly cling to her and love to seem;
Whiles I am daily waiting for sweet death,
To give me peace and put my soul to rest.

1st JAILOR.—Thy prayer has been heard, old man.

MORTARA.—What do I hear?—Is death then drawing nigh?
And may I soon be living free of pain?
O, say again I have been doomed to die,
And let me suck the honey of those words.

1st JAILOR.—Some hours ere dawn of day as I held watch,
Before the portals of this gloomy cell,
Proud Ludovico with a monk appeared,
To whom, sir, after he acquainted him,
With all the tortures thou hadst undergone,
He stated that this night,—this very night
Thou wilt be executed in the Pontiff's name.

MORTARA.—Here, harbinger of joy, upon my knees
I bless thee for the welcome tidings brought.

(MORTARA kneels.)

Hadst thou restored to me my liberty;
Mine eyes to see; my health—my strength—my home;
My wife—my child—my Jephthah—all I love,
And with them crowns and sceptres of a king,
To reign supreme upon this breathing globe,
With stores immense of gold and silver-coin;
With rubies verging into velvet:
Some carmine red; some hyacinthine hued,
And others—sapphirine and cinnabar;
With diamonds purer than contrition's tears,
And clearer than the founts of Paradise;
Each pebble fickle in transparency;

In octahedrons of a million sparks,
More bright and dazzling than the lightning's flash,
Which piercing through black cloudlets blend the earth.
Why, christian, all these treasures of the world
Tenfold increased in love and worth to me,
I would relinquish for this single word,
Which now inspires me with such happiness,
That all I suffered is at once forgot,
And nothing stirs my soul but gratitude.

(MORTARA rises.)

Slowly pass the hours of man's sojourn on earth,
Which carry on their back some rankling grief;
Each second seems a year; each year an age
Of pestering now the future to bedim.
But fleeter than the beams of yonder sun,
Are moments teeming with ecstatic bliss.
The mind then revels in unusual mirth,
And night approaches in the laugh of morn.
Thus studying to prolong the luscious joy,
We hear her say: I was—but am no more.
How swiftly will my suffering end in night,
And night despatch me to the realm of day.
Whiles I am thinking how and when I'll die,
The season's fled and I am gone to be.
Kind Jailor, where art thou?

1st JAILOR.—Here. Art thou in want of aught?

MORTARA.—Of nothing, Christian, thou canst give me.
Am I near thee?

1st JAILOR.—Thou art, old man.

MORTARA.—As this will be the last—the last of days,
And I on earth will never hear thee more,
Pray, grant me pardon ere we separate,
For troubles caused in my imprisonment.
Too oft my moans awoke thee from repose,
And filled thy mind with clamors of distress.
I have been peevish, sullen, querulous,

'Although thou only didst perform thy task.

1st JAILOR.—Kind, kind man.

MORTARA.—I am a crippled—childish—silly fool;
Thou too may'st grow as hoary as myself:
Forgive me then, good Christian, do forgive,
That when thou art as old as I, our Judge
May grant thee friends to guard thy feeble self.

1st JAILOR.—Much suffering Hebrew, how can I forgive
Offenses only living in thy mind?
Sensitive and delicate were thy ways,
And all thy words bespoke thee, Gentleman.
Old man, why dost distort thy features so?

MORTARA.—Unnatural thirst sits burning in my throat!
Come, Jailor; lead me to my mat!—I'm ill.
And have the monsters drugged my broth again?
Touch not mine arms—they're wounded—Oh, oh!

1st JAILOR.—Excuse me, sir, for my great negligence.

MORTARA.—Jailor! Have they drugged my meal?
O, monsters! monsters!

1st JAILOR.—I do not know of the ingredients used.

MORTARA.—And will they even torture me to-day?
Not give me time to bless them ere I die?
Jailor—Jailor! but a drop of water;
My throat is full of fire—O, O! what thirst!

1st JAILOR.—I can not help thee man; no water's here.

MORTARA.—What cruel, cruel treatment.—O, my throat!
Get me the juice of Scammony or such
Which purge one clean and quells devouring thirst.
Jailor! my lips—my tongue burns like a living coal.
O, give me some water——   (falls down.)
                              O, only a drop;
A single drop and Heaven will reward thee.

1st JAILOR.—I have no water for thee, poor old man,
          (*Exit* JAILOR.)

MORTARA.—O, but a single drop;—my fauces burn——
          (*Enter* CORNELIA.)

O, Jailor, pity, pity—pity me.
My breath is warmer than the fires of Hell;
My windpipe's dryer than the desert's sand.
I'm suffocating—O, O!

          (He moans and weeps aloud.)

I can't endure this lava in my throat—
My blood dissolves to smoke and stifles me,
I'm burning up;—some water, water, friend.

    (MORTARA moans and weeps; Cornelia who has been quietly watching exposes her breast, to which she places his mouth and feeds him with her milk.)

    CORNELIA.—Drink, drink, old man and quell your bitter
      thirst;
Drink, while you may and suck the nipple dry;
The milk is yours, may it allay your pains,
And give you life although it brings me death.
The breast whose office is to feed the young—
The smiling babe just ushered into life,—
Shall never still an infant of my womb,
For Jephthah's gone and I am desolate.
So drain it up, the little milk that's left;
By force it came when nature was abused.
O, gland! deny me not the gentle fluid,
But at my bidding fill my maiden-pap;
And from its eye drip tears to cool his throat,
And nourish him with milk of virginhood.

        (CORNELIA covers her breast again.)

    MORTARA.—A succoring angel hast thou been to me,
Whiles from thy heaving breast I drew fresh life.
O, how I thirsted for a kindly drop,
But who save thee would pity this old man?
I wept, I cried—as helpless as I am
They left me here to suffer and to weep.

    CORNELIA.—I feel for you.

    MORTARA.—I suffered much, my daughter;—very much.

    CORNELIA.—Who suffers not? O, power above, say who?

MORTARA.—Jehovah's merciful, my daughter.

CORNELIA.—You taught me so, old man.

MORTARA.—Believe it, daughter, believe it.

CORNELIA.—I do, old man. (She covers her face and weeps.)

MORTARA.—What is the matter with thee, daughter?

CORNELIA.—I am unhappy, father.

MORTARA.—Reach me thy hand. (MORTARA kisses her hand.)
Thy hand is cold; hast thou been sick?

CORNELIA.—I have.   (She weeps.)

MORTARA.—Come, let me kiss it, till it groweth warm.
What ailed thee, child?

CORNELIA.—O, father, father! I'm too unhappy.

MORTARA.—Pray, child, explain what has befallen thee.
Let this blind man be sharer of thy woes.
His misery increases through suspense,
So speak and quiet the agitated heart.

CORNELIA.—Father.

MORTARA.—Speak, my daughter.

CORNELIA.—I'm mad!

MORTARA.—Mad?

CORNELIA.—Mad.

MORTARA.—Let me kiss thee, my daughter.
          (CORNELIA embraces him and weeps.)
It is His will.

CORNELIA.—I murmur not. I think no more of earth.

MORTARA.—Nor I, my daughter.
A better world awaiteth us.

CORNELIA.—What would I be without that hope?

MORTARA.—Since when, my daughter, art thou ill?

CORNELIA.—Since yestermorn delirium preys on me.
This symptomatic fever in my brain
In maniac shrieks and ravings wild gave vent,
Until exhausted covered with white foam
I sank upon the floor a crazy wretch.
How long I raved, or that I raved at all,
As I awoke from what did seem a trance,

Was told me by the Jailor I espied
Within my prison standing at my side.

MORTARA.—'Tis weakness, child, and soon will pass away.

CORNELIA.—Never while I live; (she weeps) never.

MORTARA.—All troubles have an end, and why not thine?
Who knows to-day what even the morrow brings?
It is not the mortal's lot to rend the vail,
Which hideth from our view futurity.

CORNELIA.—'Tis even so, my father.

MORTARA.—Last night as memory scanned each single line,
Recorded in the volume of my brain,
And I called up a thousand trivial tales,
To cheer the sinking spirit with what's past:
I never dreampt that ere another night
Throws her black curtain o'er nature's seat,
I would be wafted to my Yulah's home,
Again to live released of mortal pain.

CORNELIA.—What heavy news does break upon my mind!
Have they resolved to torture you to death?
To send you hence ere nature's satisfied?
Will they besmear with gore these silver threads?
Perhaps with irons drive your spirit forth?
It makes me mad to think on't!—mad!

MORTARA.—Have no anxiety, my daughter.

CORNELIA.—Father! what must Cornelia do?

MORTARA.—Pray, my daughter, pray.

CORNELIA.—I will.   (She weeps.)

MORTARA.—Dry up thy tears.

CORNELIA.—I can not, father.

MORTARA.—Immaculate spirit!   God of Israel!
Mankind's friend! have pity on thy supplicant;
O, look down and hear the old man's prayer:
I do entreat thee, let thy trials end;
O, spare this maid and let her feel thy Grace.
Restore her reason and her liberty.
Jehovah! she hath been so kind to me,

Whose winter teemed with unabated storms.
Reward her then, O Judge, with earth or heaven.

CORNELIA.—O, father, father!

    (She falls down before him and weeps.)

MORTARA.—Weep not, my daughter.

CORNELIA.—O, how can I such wild emotions soothe,
When consolation parteth in your doom?
As long as I beheld your fortitude
My soul forgot all grief and misery.
But now this pattern is withdrawn from me,
And I must grope alone this life's long road.

MORTARA.—Not so my daughter. God is ever nigh.
Make him thy steward; aye, thy confident;
Confess to Him and let Him know thy grief.
Each tear that falleth in thy doing so,
But lightens all thy cares and stills thy soul.
No need of human aid when He befriends.
His thoughts are deeds—be worthy of that thought.

CORNELIA.—I am resigned, my father.

MORTARA.—'Tis well. Now lead me to my mat.

CORNELIA.—But for one moment let me close mine eyes.
I'll help thee instantly, my father.
I'm dizzy;—hold me—everything swims;
Father!   (CORNELIA glaring wildly 'round the cell.)

MORTARA.—I can not see thee, daughter.

CORNELIA.—Father!   (With a maniac laugh.)

MORTARA.—Cornelia, my child, speak.

CORNELIA.—I'm mad. (She jumps up; heaves and foams.)
Spare him!—spare him! let me be punished!
Mine's the crime!   (Followed by a wild laugh.)
Not heed me?—not listen to me?—you must!
Holy Pontiff! would you harm the old man?
Do it you dare!—do it.   (Laughs frantically.)

MORTARA, (trying to approach her.)—What means this in-
  coherent rant, my child?

CORNELIA.—Ha, ha! art here?

(Seizing MORTARA around his neck.)

Have I got thee at last?

(She laughs wildly, whiles MORTARA wails.)

MORTARA.—O, let me loose.—My breast, oh! my breast.

CORNELIA.—Pontiff! where's Jephthah? where's Jephthah?
Ha ha, would you kill Mortara?—you would?

MORTARA.—Delirious maid!—Heaven! she kills me.

CORNELIA.—Release him! not?—not release him?
Pontiff! take this!—Ha, ha, ha.

(She laughs wildly; deals him a blow in the face, and jerks
him to the ground.)

Now Pontiff! who is the victor?—who?

Cornelia! (Hurries up and down the room with a frantic
laugh.)

Enter 1ST JAILOR.

JAILOR.—What's here?—Cornelia?—and mad?
Let's seize her; see how she foams!

MORTARA.—Harm her not; she's—she's—(faints.)

JAILOR.—Look! how weak she grows!—she falls.

(CORNELIA falls into the arms of JAILOR who carries her off.)

SCENE 4TH.—A ROOM IN ABRAHAM'S DWELLING.

Enter ABRAHAM, JEPHTHAH, JUDAH and LEON.

JEPHTHAH.—Two years elapsed since I took leave of you,
Expecting never more to breathe in Rome.
Grave circumstances wrought within that time,
Annulled the resolution and here I am.
'Twere folly now to weep o'er water spilt;
To argue and to chafe o'er what is done;
To accuse me even of pale cowardice—
Of fear—of want of courage if you will:
It would not give us back the friends we've lost;
No, nor the time that saw them carried off.
The present moment must decide for us,
And rob the past of her unlawful claims.
The world is silent to the wrongs of Rome,

12

Nought has been done to benefit the Jew
If legislation won't give us our rights;
Why, who dare blame us for the force applied.
Judah, my friend, a world of thanks are thine,
For thy unceasing efforts in our cause.
To thee we are indebted for this trail
Thy wariness and prudence found at last;
The password to Mortara's prison-house;
The cell wherein young Benjamin is kept;
The edict of the Pope to slay mine uncle:
For all these informations, thousand thanks.

    JUDAH.—Ever true and noble Jephthah.

    JEPHTHAH.—Come, friends, and hear our plan
Delay is hugging fatal consequence,
With strange effects to mar our bold design.
You, my teacher seek the Tiber's shore,
The boat have ready and the sailor's nigh.
And thou, my Leon, stay our sentinel,
Whiles Judah and myself steal Benjamin,
With whom ye straight must leave the capitol,
And place him in the hands of Abraham.
I soon will join you with Mortara;
But if I come not ere the hour of ten,
Sail on, my friends, and pray for Jephthah's soul.

    ABRAHAM.—O, hear me, Jephthah, nor dismay my words
I was thy teacher and thy father's friend;
Mortara loved me with a brother's love,
And many favors has he shown to me.
My wife and children all deplore the man.
How oft I wept—how oft I cried aloud,
Let Heaven record who saw the million tears.

    JEPHTHAH.—Prithee man, be more sententious.

    ABRAHAM.—Too rash and easy tickled youth, take heed,
And follow not thy splenitive desires.
Have deference for a more experienced head,
Who warns thee to engage not wildly thus.

Thy plan's ill-matured and of no avail.
Doubly must success attend an enterprise,
Ere heels can carry out the mind's design.
If thou wouldst save thine uncle and his son,
Betray them not to deeper misery.
Should fortune frown at thy too bold attempt,
Then son and sire are sentenced in thy fate.
But since Jehovah wills Mortara's death,
Let's be resigned and wish him speedy flight.
'Tis better far to live in heaven than here;
What pleasures can the blind man have on earth?
None, none, unless it groweth out of woe.
He suffered much, let him now go to sleep:
The blind, the tortured, flayed and thirsty sage.

JEPHTHAH.—Give pardon, teacher, if mine uncouth words
Bespoke me rude and ill-advised withal;
I thought them trimmed to suit the purpose well.
If they did smack of chiding disrespect;
Of silly orders of still sillier plans:
'Twas love and duty which impelled me on,
To speak and do the thing I have avowed.

ABRAHAM.—I counsel thee, to further not this plan.
Which must but end disastrously to us.
Thy sky-claimed uncle has been too abused;
His eyes put out—his hands and arms all flayed.
In short he's now a burthen to himself.
Why, then to drag him from his prisonment,
(Could even such a thing be done—I doubt it much,)
'Twere only to prolong his sufferings.
Now heed my words—despise them not unweighed.
Suppose we could release him and escape,
We'd give the Pontiff cause to raise his voice
Against our people and against our church.
Then persecution would uplift her sword,
To slay a million for this single man.
And not a child but what would curse the hour,

Which made thee mad to rage a foolish war.
Now hear what follows should we not succeed;
Should interception raise a stumbling block:
The grave now yawning for Mortara's frame,
Would either claim thee and thy followers
For your endeavors to withhold her share,
Or tortures worse than e'er thine uncle felt.
Would be the penalty of unripe haste.
Besides the hope so potent in our mind,
That yet the Pontiff will give up the boy,
By this one act will grow an absurd myth,
And Benjamin for ever will be lost.
From such revolt—such war 'gainst reason self,
My voice dissuades.

    LEON.—'T is true, our nation may condemn such plots.

    JEPHTHAH.—Let those condemn, who choose a fawning life;
I'd rather live in hell, than be a cringing slave,
That Rome may spit upon my servile brow,
And I must thank her for the honor shown.
By Jehovah! is Israel's courage dead?
Is not a single spark within her breast
That crieth: up! brave warriors of the east!
Assert your rights and be yourselves again.
Are these the men that shook the world of old,
And fought against oppression with a tiger's wrath?
Who conquered Syria and her soldiery,
Who fled with terror at our phalanxes?
I tell you, teacher, Israel only sleeps;
She's still the same—the paragon of strength!
Arouse her pride,—her dignity—her worth,
And courage like a re-born Hercules,
Will raise her arm and conquer her just rights.

    JUDAH.—O, may that time be near.

    JEPHTHAH.—The narrow minded world shall know our
      trance is broke;
That Israel is her own emancipationist.

The aid denied by man, Jehovah gives;
What force did rob—man's cunning shall regain.
Each beast received a weapon of defence;
We use the one we learned in servitude.
If 'tis too weak and we must fall this night:
How many fiery youths of our great tribes
Will follow our example to set free
The victims of the Pope or die like us.
And then when prejudice exists no more,
And time recorded Israel's worth and struggles;
How her few men regained their liberty,
Or died attempting to emancipate their race:
A blush should rise upon the face of man,
To read the story of the Hebrew's fall;
And mock withal the nineteenth century,
Which boasts of freedom and Christianity—
Of light—of science—liberality;
Although a single man—Italia's curse,—
Could rob the Hebrew mother of her babe,
And quietly was allowed to keep the theft.
Where not a potentate thought it worth while
To buckle on his armor and to fight;
To show his virtue by opposing wrong,
And give assistance to a handful men,
Who have been injured by a mighty foe.

    JUDAH.—I'd be ever at thy side.

    ABRAHAM.—Pluck not the apple ere it mellow grows;
Fill not the stomach with untimely fruit;
Teach not the sire as long as thou art child;
Wield not a weapon heavier than thyself;
Ne'er cause a quarrel where there is no gain;
Oppose no foe who's stronger than thyself;
Note what man speaks, but never speak thyself;
Approve their course, yet shun their erring ways;
Crawl in the dust if dangers walk erect;
Be coward when the hero's fate is death;

12*

Show courage only when it can succeed;
Unconscious seem to wrongs thou canst not cure;
Be ever wary while the others sleep;
Seem ever drowsy to an enemy;
Stake not thy all upon a single game;
Haste not the time, for time is haste itself;
Use not thy sword, when thou canst gain in peace:
Therefore, kind friends, allay your stubborn rage,
And save from woe our people and ourselves.
The time shall come, when God will show us Grace,
And help us to regain our privilege.
I do exhort ye, friends, apply no force;
Your speculation is as wild as dangerous.
Desist, I pray you all, desist.

JUDAH.—We live not in the age of miracles;
A practicable world is this in sooth.

JEPHTHAH.—Unless we try, we never can succeed;
To lay supinely on our stiffened backs,
And wait for chance to bring us liberty:
Shows us unworthy of the boon of boons——
The rich reward of heroes and of men.

ABRAHAM.—I do implore you, ere it is too late.

JEPHTHAH.—What say you, friends?

LEON.—We suffered wrongs and should now be redressed
Yet Abraham is old and Wisdom's his.

JEPHTHAH.—Well—well——

LEON.—If Jephthah's mind is fixed;—I'll follow it.
And nothing but black death shall part me from him.

JUDAH.—Me needst not ask.
What we begun, a dastard only shuns.

JEPHTHAH.—Ha, ha! Your hands.
Now swear to cease not to advance our cause;
If one should fall think but of gain not loss.
There is a providence to guide the brave—
The coward is the firstling of the grave.
Then let's be bold—as strong as hardened steel.

Since we now fight for God and Israel's weal.
Record your oaths; I give my word in pledge,
If I do flinch, let Hell receive this wretch.
Come and swear.

    ABRAHAM.—Stop.
Since my advice has fallen to the ground,
To Heaven or hell with you I mean to mount.
Here by my beard, though wisdom could not guide,
I swear to be more bold than Absalom to-night.
'Tis true I'm old and am not strong as ye,
Yet Cæsar has been worried by a flea.

    JEPHTHAH.—Since strength and cunning now agree,
Of danger is our pathway free.
Now swear my friends; to God and Israel true;
We ask no boot, nor will we favors sue.
Swear!

    ALL.—We swear.   (They hold up their hands.)
    [*End of 4th Act.*]

ACT FIFTH.

SCENE 1ST.—CORNELIA'S CELL IN THE INQUISITION.

Enter LUDOVICO, friar LAWRENCE and JAILOR.

    LUDOVICO.—Can it be possible that loss of milk
Of her unmothered breast has crazed her mind?

    LAWRENCE.—'Tis no less possible than true.
The mind impaired through such proceedings will,
In consequence of lacking unity
Within the system of adjusted self,
Become delirious. The emulsive fluid
Thus drawn from out the breast 'scaped not the gland
By the unanimous assistance of
Her functions concentrated from all parts.
But by appeal to her imagination
Either in behalf of help-imploring pity.
Or to supply her amorous demands,
Exclusive of the body's willingness,

Has strained the mind with force to such excess,
That from her labors sprung the milk's discharge.
So stretched imagination leaping Nature's bounds,
Reduced in strength soars out of Reason's reach,
Traversing regions of bewilderment.

LUDOVICO.—Hast never found, good friar Lawrence,
Within thy many years of tedious search,
A root or herb that's potent to restore
To minds diseased their pure and pristine health.

LAWRENCE.—Such drugs I do possess, and wondrous is
Their power to re-invigorate the mind,
Whose sickness is not idiopathic.
But intellect impaired from infancy
Is not within the pale of earthly cure;
Or brains, whose wild delirium has been caused
By troubles preying deeply on the heart,
Whose memory looking in the face of grief
Shrank frightened back to close the eye of thought:
Such madness, monk, no antidote of mine
Can from the mind o'ercharged obliterate.
But where is the patient?

LUDOVICO.—Bring her in.   (JAILOR *Exit*)
We were compelled, so fierce she grew since morn,
To clothe her in the strait-gown of the mad.

LAWRENCE.—Canst thou not guess, what could have caused
     the wretch
To seek her nipple and to draw her milk,
If she in virtue lived as ye report?

LUDOVICO.—We do suspect her much of having fed,
Without our will or knowledge with her milk,
For some four weeks a hoary inmate of this jail.
But ho! (JAILOR calling loudly within) what noise?
Her hands are tied——

Enter JAILOR *in haste.*

JAILOR.—My chief!

LUDOVICO.—Speak!—if thou hast a tongue!

JAILOR.—She is not in the cell.

LUDOVICO.—What say'st thou?—not there?

JAILOR.—I searched her cell from nook to nook.
She has escaped.

LUDOVICO.—Where are the jailors all?—ring the bell!
And make each watch seek for the maniac.

(JAILOR strikes the bell.)

Come friar, let us stir the lazy sentinels.

Enter PEDROLDA and INQUISITORS.

PEDROLDA.—Why strikes the bell alarm?

LUDOVICO.—Away and search! the crazy wretch is fled.

(*Exit* ALL. The bell keeps on ringing.)

———

SCENE 2D.—BEFORE THE INQUISITION.

Enter JEPHTHAH, ABRAHAM, JUDAH, LEON—attired in friars'
habiliments.

JEPHTHAH.—Here we part. Our valiant Leon keeps us
watch.
You, most reverend sire, go now toward the shore,
Our ever-faithful Judah and myself
Shall traverse instantly, as we have planned,
The secret passage leading to the Pope,
And to our suffering kin.—So fare you well.

ABRAHAM.—Be wary, youth, and our success is sure.

JEPHTHAH.—I have hearkened to your counsel.

ABRAHAM.—And should we never meet again on earth ——

JUDAH.—Let Israel's God unite our souls in Heaven.

LEON.—It is my heartfelt wish.

JEPHTHAH.—Amen. 'Tis mine, I swear it.
Prithee, on your mission now;—'tis growing late.

ABRAHAM.—A last and fond embrace.

JEPHTHAH.—Here's to success.—O, sacred privilege!
To shed the solid tear upon your trusty breast.

ABRAHAM.—May'st thou not fall a sacrifice.—Adieu to all.

JUDAH.—We'll meet again.

LEON.—Upon the Tiber's strand.—Await us there.

ABRAHAM.—Adieu.

Jephthah——

JEPHTHAH.—No more.
Commend me to my people if I fall.
(*Exit* ABRAHAM.)
Leon, if sentinels should question thee,
Whiles we are gone to lure the boy away:
" From whence thou camest, or who thou waitest for "——
Tell them thou art a friar of St. Lutzen,
And that thou art in stay of certain monks,
Whom holy Pius honored with an audience.

JUDAH.—Keep in the dark as much as possible,
And if some strangers should come loitering here,
Disperse them in the name of Ludovico.

LEON.—Brave friends, pray have no troubles on my score.
I will be cautious in my watch.

JEPHTHAH.—Now get thee somewhat out of sight.
Adieu.

JUDAH.—Be near when we approach.—Good-bye.

LEON.—Adieu.   (*Exit* LEON.)

JEPHTHAH.—Come on my guard, I'll follow thee to death;
The boy we'll free, or lose to-night our breath.
Jehovah! if our cause be just and right,
Approve it in my cousin's speedy flight.
(*Exit* JEPHTHAH and JUDAH.)

SCENE 3D.—A PASSAGE IN THE INQUISITION.
Enter JAILORS and INQUISITORS.   Alarm.

1ST JAILOR.—This way, my friends; this way.

2D JAILOR.—I can't imagine how she did escape.

3D JAILOR.—Nor I.   Her hands were tied and her cell well-
barred.

1ST JAILOR.—Analyze this question at some other time;
Our duty now is: searching for the maniac.

3D JAILOR.—I hear some one approach; —'t is Cornelia——

1ST JAILOR.—'T is the holy father of St. Lutzen that approaches.

Enter JEPHTHAH' and JUDAH.

Most holy gentlemen, have ye not seen,
Or heard as ye advanced, a furious wretch—
A crazy woman, who escaped her cell,
And now has fled, we know not whither?

JUDAH.—How was she dressed, my sons?

1ST JAILOR.—She wears a strait-jacket.

JUDAH.—Such a woman have we seen, like an arrow,
Shooting down the lane, that leadeth to the capitol.

1ST JAILOR.—Were handcuffs placed around her wrist?

JUDAH.—If I mistake not;—yes, my sons.

1ST JAILOR.—Let's after her.

2D JAILOR.—And quickly too, else we'll lose the track.
(*Exit* JAILORS and INQUISITORS.)

JUDAH.—Heaven be praised for this timed accident,
Which almost leaves us masters of these cells.
Come, my Jephthah—this is Benjamin's.
(JUDAH knocks at the door of that cell.)

JAILOR, (within.)—Who knocks.

JUDAH.—A man with the cross.

JAILOR, (within.)—Whither away so late?

JUDAH.—To trail the fox.

JAILOR, (within.)—The pass is clear——

JUDAH.—To the man of the cross.
(The door opens, and JUDAH and JEPHTHAH *enter.*)

*Enter Cornelia with a maniac laugh; her hair disheveled, hanging in
wild disorder over her neck; wearing a strait-jacket, also handcuffs
appended to a long iron chain reaching the ground.*

CORNELIA.—Why, Pontiff! Jephthah's innocent!—I lured
    him on.
Have you the heart to kill him?—take my nipple:
Drink old man—what! mad?—who says, I'm mad?
Who says—you lie—he must not die for me.
For me? have mercy, mercy—O! have—wretch!
He has white hair—so gentle—ha, ha! he's free!
Won't you come back to me, Jephthah?—thou art a Jew—

They're after me—let go—I'll kill thee, Pius!

(She takes the iron chain and strikes it on the ground.)

Ha, ha! Mortara's free!—the Pope is dead.——hist;

My mother's here—O, my mother—sainted mother!

(She sinks upon her knees and lifts her hands heavenward.)

Let me weep upon thy breast, my mother;　(weeps,)

They say I'm mad—mad—mad;　(muses for a while.)

(Sings.)　　　　　　SONG.

> My mother dear, I call thy name;
> 　Forsake me not—thy child:
> Come, mother dear, thy daughter claim;
> 　I know thou art so mild.

Where am I?—flee, my Jephthah—do I love him?

My heart—my brain,——'twas I who saved him, Pontiff!

I'm crazy, good, old father;—I am resigned——

(Sings.)　　From the lattice down the rocks
> 　　Leaps he in the sea below;
> Gory shake his raven locks
> 　　Nightly on the river Po.
> Perjured maid, his ghost is here,
> 　　Ghost is here;
> Claiming thee to fill his bier—
> 　　Fill his bier.

Will they kill him to night?—Love thee, Jephthah?

Love thee?　Ha, ha!　Cornelia struck thee dead!

Who art thou?　　　　　　　　　　(She rises.)

> Hast seen my Jephthah?—how is he?

Beautiful?—the Pope—I'll sing; shall I, my love?

(Sings.)　　When at morn the green meadows were weeping
> 　　Their bright tear-pearls a-gleaming like stars,
> I would bound and would dance and be leaping,
> 　　With a glow on my dimples like Mars;
> 　　With a glow on my dimples like Mars.

What are these? (looking at the handcuffs) ha, ha!

My wedding ring!—Jephthah gave it to me.

I'm coming—go on—　　　　(the bell rings.　Alarm.)

They kill him—I'll save thee—ha, ha!

(CORNELIA runs out.)

SCENE 4TH.—BEFORE THE INQUISITION.

Enter LEON.

LEON.—What means this loud alarm?—this boisterous peal?
This hurrying to and fro of these inquisitors?
They should be here and yet I hear no steps.
An hour slipped hence since they have left me here.
Can they have been apprised?—methinks I hear——
List! yes, yes; they're coming—

Enter JUDAH.

How is it?—speak!

JUDAH.—A curse upon them! they recognized both of us.
Hark each sentinel is awake and on our track.

(A terrible noise within; the bells toll loudly.)

They must have cut off his retreat!—hear!—swords!

Enter JEPHTHAH *with* BENJAMIN *on his arms.*

JEPHTHAH, (bleeding; his sword besmeared with blood.)—
Take him.

Pray, instantly flee with him to the Tiber's shore.

JUDAH.—What wouldst thou do?

JEPHTHAH.—Release mine uncle.

JUDAH.—Thou canst not; hark!—a thousand spies
Are on our track!—flee with us.

JEPHTHAH.—Your oaths!—remember your oaths!

JUDAH.—We all are lost, if we a moment stay.

JEPHTHAH.—Go quickly with your precious charge; I bid!
Else this my sword shall pierce your traitorous hearts.

JUDAH.—Adieu.—Come Benjamin.

(*Exit* JUDAH, LEON *and* BENJAMIN.)

JEPHTHAH.—God bless you, kindest friends.
Now Heaven assist me to release this sage;
I feel a lion in my bosom rage.

(*Exit* JEPHTHAH.)

———

SCENE 5TH.—A ROOM IN THE PONTIFF'S PALACE.

Enter PONTIFF, LUDOVICO *and* JAILOR.

PIUS.—No more. By St. Peter has it come to this?

13

Are we no longer safe in Rome?—Vipers!
This smacks of treachery!—ha, ha, Ludovico!
Officer! art thou sure 'twas Jephthah?
Hast thou seen him with thine own eyes?

JAILOR.—I have, your Grace.

PIUS.—And thou dost live to tell us that he fled?
Accursed be thy soul, thou honey-sucking loon!

JAILOR.—Your Grace——

PIUS.—Get thee out of our sight;—we're sick to look at
thee!

(Exit JAILOR.*)*

Where were our Jailors and Inquisitors,
Not to perceive these strangers in the vault?

LUDOVICO.—Cornelia, who has grown delirious, sire,
Escaped from out her prisonment this night;
Upon her track Inquisitor and Jailor went.

PIUS.—Recall them! This Jephthah must they find,
Else shall these hirelings feel the penalty of death.
Let every bell peal thunders o'er Rome!
Rebellion stalks abroad——what now!

Enter OFFICER.

Is Jephthah caught?—speak but that single word,
And we will plant thee higher than a king.

OFFICER.—Your Grace! Benjamin, the novice——

PIUS.—What of him?—has he revealed the plot?

OFFICER.—No, no; your Grace——

PIUS.—What then?

OFFICER.—He fled!

PIUS.—Break off thy damned tale; it makes us wild!
Benjamin fled and Jephthah back in Rome?
By St. Peter! is it this we labored for?
Does Heaven and hell conspire against our Grace?
Arouse each sentinel!—let every cell be searched!
Imprison every Jew!—lock up our gates!
Why stare at us?—begone, ye drowsy slaves!

(Exit LUDOVICO and OFFICER.*)*

Audacious Jew! bold and lion-mettled knave!
We'll pamper in thy death this very night;
Long hast thou kept our power at bay;—but now
The drama closes and the feast begins.
We can't await the moment on whose back
This impious wretch is carried like a knave
Into our presence.—What, ho! who's here?

Enter JEPHTHAH, (muffled.)

Who art thou, priest, intruding at this hour?

JEPHTHAH.—A person at whose name the Pontiff trembles.

PIUS.—Unmask thyself, and let me read thy face.

JEPHTHAH.—Death quivers on my lips and poisonous is my
breath.

PIUS.—Speak, strange visitor! what wouldst thou have?

JEPHTHAH.—Thy life.

PIUS.—Who art thou?— speak!

JEPHTHAH.—Mastai Ferrett's evil genius.   Wouldst know
more?

PIUS.—Mysterious man!—so dreadful to my sight——
What e'er thy mission give it breath!

JEPHTHAH.—I can not.

PIUS.—And why?

JEPHTHAH.—My mission taketh breath.

PIUS.—Who e'er thou art, man—demon—fiend of hell!
Show me thy face and let me know thy want.

JEPHTHAH, (unmuffling.)—My name is Jephthah.

PIUS.—Begone; begone——leave our sight.
I'd rather hug a viper to my breast,
Than have thee near me.—Avaunt! avaunt!

JEPHTHAH.—Long hast thou searched for me;—what wouldst
thou now?
I'm here.

PIUS.—If thou dost love thy life: begone at once,
Else like a scorpion will I have thee crushed.

JEPHTHAH.—I wait upon thy patience.

PIUS, (drawing a dagger.)—Wretch!

JEPHTHAH.—Hold! (tearing the dagger out of Pius' hands.)
Mastai Ferrett deals not with a child.

PIUS.—We do command thee, go.

JEPHTHAH.—Thou didst command me to come.

PIUS.—What can we do to get thee out of sight?

JEPHTHAH, (taking hold of his neck.)—Mastai Ferrett.

PIUS.—Have mercy; O, have mercy.

JEPHTHAH.—Mercy?—and why should I have mercy?
Why should I spare the life, which if it could
Annihilate high Heaven's chosen race,
Would like a wolf leap on the tender prey,
Without remorse—without compunction's sting,
That it could feast upon their blood?—Mercy?
What hast thou done with Benjamin, the novice?
His cheek looks pallid and his eye is sunk?
Why wast thou deaf? couldst no entreaties hear?
And kepst him from his mother and his sire?
Wretch! that mother who could not survive the loss,
Now buried lies a victim of thy work.
In Heaven she smiling does behold thee now
Receive thy dues——

PIUS.—Thou stiflest me.

JEPHTHAH.—Where is mine uncle—the harmless, honest
man?
What has he done that thou keep'st him locked up?
Is it for his industry—for his peace,
At home—abroad—with strangers or with friends,
That thou didst torture him in his old age?
I left him in the autumn of his life
Awaiting Heaven appeased with God and man;
Golden smiles were playing on his brow;
His silver hair would melt the heart to love,
And through his eyes a gentle welcome laughed,
That, tigers looking, would have been subdued.
Yet thou, vile wretch, couldst steel thy heart withal,
And make it harder far than Adamant.

Where was thy pity when thou madest him blind?
Where was thy mercy whiles he felt thy rack?
A million wasps didst fatten with his blood!
Thou didst deny him even a single drop
To quench his bitter thirst. O, shame!—fie! fie!
Hast not been taught to show respect to age?
To be his staff and make his journey light?
To sing his life away and close his eyes?
Or, is't thy faith to persecute the old?
To rack, to burn, to flay, to thirst them dead!
Why, hellish demon! guilty art thou found
In the face of Heaven and earth. And yet
This very night thou wouldst have slain mine uncle.

    Pius.—Let loose thy hold and he shall be released.
Thy gripe upon my throat is stifling me.

    Jephthah.—Hand me the bull tied to a silken thread,
As emblem of thy Grace to spare his life.
Quickly, else my dagger finds thy heart.

    Pius.—Upon yon wall the edict hangs: ·
If thou canst reach so high, obtain the thing.

    Jephthah.—Were it as high as Heaven itself, I'd pull it
      down.

(He walks toward the wall, and as he pulls the edict down,
      Pius shoots at him and wounds him.)

O, fatal shot! Mortara dies in me.

(Noise without. Pius tries to run toward the door but is in-
      tercepted by Jephthah.)

Hold!
What edict else have I to take along,
As herald of so great a potentate.
Speak quickly, sir, each moment's now an age
Of misery and woe. I'm growing faint;
The blood is flowing from my heart; I feel
A chill creep o'er me;—it is the chill of death,
And yet Mortara—hearest not the noise?
They come—thy hirelings!—what edict else?
   13*

Pius.—Help! O, help!

Jephthah.—What edict else? Quickly sing it out!

Pius.—None.—Help!—ha, ha! they're coming!

Jephthah.—To find thee dead.   (Stabs him.)
To hell and meet thy predecessors.

        (Pius falls.)

Pius.—There's comfort; thou must follow me.
I'm dying——   (dies.)

Jephthah.—A happier death is mine to see and know,
Mortara freed—thyself to Pluto go.
O, let me live mine uncle to restore;
'Tis all I ask this side of Heaven's shore.

        (*Exit* Jephthah.)

Scene 6th.—Inside of the Inquisition.
Enter Jephthah *with a drawn sword.*

Jephthah.—O, Hope! this wound is calling out my life,
And I grow feeble through the loss of blood.
Yet will I on, nor stop to rest my bones,
Until this orphan's duty is performed.
On! on!   (*Exit* Jephthah.)

Enter Cornelia.

Cornelia.—Out! out! the Pontiff has escaped me. Out!
Make room! Hell's charioteer rides through the wind!

        (*Exit* Cornelia.)

Scene 7th.—Mortara's cell in the Inquisition.
Present—*Two Inquisitors engaged racking the fingers of Mortara's hands, whiles a third holds a pan of hot oil. Pedrolda, Cardinal Savelli, Bishop Bedini and Inquisitors.*

Mortara.—My tongue is sealed. Keep on your tortures
    then.
These hands shall rather rot from off the wrists,
Ere speech of mine betrays a sign of fear.
Pinch harder—aye, mash and squeeze the flesh;
I am indifferent to man's woes and pangs.

SAVELLI.—Try the virtue of the steaming oil.

(The Inquisitors raise MORTARA's arm, o'er which the oil is poured.)

MORTARA.—O, O, what pain.

SAVELLI.—These pangs and worse than such thy son shall feel,

Unless this night thou bend'st thy stubborn will,

And answerest us the query we proposed.

Drop your instrument.—Support him.

(Inquisitors drop their instruments.)

MORTARA.—If 'tis Jehovah's will that he should suffer:

The infant he entrusted to my care;

The boy who often sat upon my knee:

Although I love him with a father's love,

And would deliver up my life for his,

Yet is my brother's son as dear to me,

Who near my heart long since took up a seat:

I would not sacrifice the orphaned youth,

To save my Benjamin from woe—from death.

SAVELLI.—Inform his Grace through us, where Jephthah fled;

How we may find him and bring back withal,

To stand his trial in the courts of Rome.

And then the Pontiff in his clemency

For this great service done to church and state,

Will give thee straight thy long-lost liberty;

Return thy son to comfort thy last days;

Possess thee of thy confiscated wealth,

And make amends for all thy miseries,

For all the tortures thou didst undergo.

Physicians crowned with practice and with lore;

The skilled of Italy will he engage,

To heal thy wounds—these lacerated arms:

To quell thy thirst—invigorate thy breast;

Infuse throughout thy blood its wonted fire

That in thy lot thou might'st forget the past.

But if thou'rt deaf to all this lenity
And wilt reveal not this young rebel's lair—
The place — the town—the country whence he fled,
Hear through Savelli what his grace commands:
It is his word (and we obey his laws)
To rack thy son and burn his eyeballs out;
To flay his feet and make him walk on sand;
To roast his flesh and lay him on crushed glass;
To free his teeth and irritate the gum;
To drive thin splinters in his joints, and have
Him dance upon a sheet of heated iron.
Then will we make a target of his breast,
And try our skill to miss the vital spot.
What say'st thou to thy offspring's doom?

MORTARA.—What can I say?—I can't but weep.

SAVELLI.—And thee we are commanded to destroy,
By cleaving thy white head in twain.

MORTARA.—His will be done.

     (He falls on his knees and bends his head.)

SAVELLI.—Once more we ask thee for thy choice.

MORTARA.—I have said.

SAVELLI.—Take up the axe, and when this bell strikes ten.
Let me behold thee split Mortara's head.
Art ready?

INQUISITOR.—I am, most holy Cardinal.

     (The bell strikes nine times; a noise heard.)

SAVELLI.—What noise is this?

JEPHTHAH, (without.)—Away, away!
Who dares impede the Pontiff's messenger?
Let loose, sentinel! of moment is my presence!
Hold! hold! I bring a pardon of his Grace,
Die, wretch! I came not in a playful mood.

     Enter JEPHTHAH, staggering.

Here! here!
The Pontiff's seal tied to a silken thread!

     (He hands it to Savelli.)

Mortara.—I hear my Jephthah! where art thou, my boy?
(Mortara rises and Jephthah means to embrace him but falls
down before him.)

Jephthah.—I'm here.

Mortara.—Where art thou my boy?

(He seeks him—then kneels down behind him.)

Jephthah.—I'm dying uncle;—thou art free—leave me.

Mortara.—I can not see thee, my boy.

Jephthah.—Thy Benjamin is free and safe—free.

Mortara.—My Benjamin saved?   (dies.)

Jephthah.—How dark all seems before me;—how dark—
What do I hear—hark!

Cornelia, (without, sings.)

> From the lattice down the rocks
> > Leaps he in the sea below;
> Gory shake his raven locks
> > Nightly on the river Po.
> Perjured maid, his ghost is here,
> > Ghost is here;
> Claiming thee to fill his bier—

(*Enter* Cornelia singing)   Fill his bier.

Jephthah, (jumping up.)—I know that voice——

Cornelia, (staring at him, shrieks.)—It is—it is my Jephthah.   (She falls down and dies)

Jephthah.—Dead? dead?   (kneels down to kiss her.)
I come—I come—I——   (He dies.)

(A strain of mournful music.)

END OF MORTARA TRAGEDY.

CHOICE POEMS.

BY H. M. MOOS.

The Struggle of Despair.

Who whispers here! he left poor Madelaine?
  Who dares to charge him with that horrid deed?
Who will from such abuses not refrain?
  Who thinks that anger can't to curses lead?—
Though plucked the flower, he'll not destroy the weed,
  Which made him live when he himself is dead.
He'll come again, poor Madelaine to greet;
  Will dry her tears, then make her smile instead,
  And heal the wound—the heart which for him bled.

Can he have left me thus? No, no! O, no!
  'Twere more than cruel to forsake me here,
And leave me in this place of shame and woe,
  Where none, save victims of deceit appear.—
I see him now—methinks a pearly tear
  Now, gem-like, sparkles in his eagle-eyes;
For none, not e'en poor Madelaine, is near,
  To share his grief, and mingle sighs with sighs,
  Infusing hope, which Fate, to yearning hearts, denies.

Ye murmuring winds! what know ye of my love?
  Have ye not met him on your onward flight?
Sends he no words to his despairing dove?
  Bring ye no sigh from my too far off guide,
As proof of his not yet forgotten plight?
  Has he not told you of poor Madelaine?
(His joy by day—his only dream by night,)
  How she has loved him, till her maddening brain
  Was filled with naught, save whom she loved in vain.

The winds howl on, and shake each drooping leaf,
 Which, shivering, hears of Madelaine's despair:
The lofty oak now seems enwrapped in grief,
 While rattling storm sweeps moaning through the air
Dispersing clouds, for tidings none they bear.
 The angry sea—now each unruly wave
Commandeth her a blacker aspect wear;
 The bird on high—wild beast in frowning cave,
 Seem filled with gloom, for much-wronged love does rave.

E'en here I'll hope's untimely death deplore;
 Fond Hope! which in my bosom rankling dies;
And send my plaints o'er surging ocean's shore,
 Recalling from abroad my love with sighs;
His image still within my bosom lies;
 His stately form I dare behold no more;
Afar, afar, I fix my searching eyes,
 And hear the disagreeing waters roar,
 On billows black: "In vain thou didst this main explore."

The lofty oak—the modest, sighing reed—
 The sliding stream—the warbling rivulet—
The gushing spring—unfathomed ocean's seat,
 And whispering breeze to answer seemed to dread,
But onward with my hope their echo sped.
 Then come Remorse! and torture Madelaine;
Dethrone her reason—waning Hope has fled;
 Come Madness! come! destroy her thinking brain,
 And be alleviator of his mental pain.

For now he basketh in some radiant smile,
 Which on deluded victim's dimples plays;
And whispers tales of love, but to beguile
 The tedious minutes as they onward chase.
Now, his enamored, melting, winning gaze,
 Stern Virtue lures from consecrated bower;
Then, fear and caution's penetrating rays,

He charms with thrilling speeches from their tower,
And leaves Desire alone, its tempted self to cower.

If I had lost a home and all the pleasures,
  With which, on earth, my bloomy rise was blessed;
Or Fate denied me Mammon's golden treasures;
  Or never felt the bliss to be caressed
By friends, who dare make love thus manifest;
  Or thorns were strewn on every path I'd tread;
Or illness were my everlasting guest;
  And every hour more sorrows would beget;
  I still could live, or leave this world without regret.

But, worse than these, to pine away in shame,
  And meet with none who pities me on earth;
Though friends I had, ere yet the tempter came
  As curse to me and those who gave me birth,
Installing grief and choke the voice of mirth.
  Yet, I am hated, for I loved too well,
Not he who lured me from my father's hearth:
  Nor tear they shed for her who, trusting, fell
  From Virtue's shrine, into abyss of scorching hell.

In limits none, their censure they confine,
  But, unrestrained, give vent, when me they meet:
" Here walks the harlot (or the concubine,)
  Who left her home a lewder life to lead,
And looks sedate now hide her lusty deed."
  O Gods! too keen for me, this punishment;
That horrid name, let them no more repeat: —
  I am defenceless, maids! then curses send
  As thick as hail on her who can't resent.

Though now dishonored, yet not honorless,
  Nor senseless, so as not to feel the wound
Inflicted on the fallen motherless —
  Oh! were she buried 'neath the self-same ground
Where parents loved, eternal rest have found;

And slept in peace until, on judgment day,
Great Jove, his council holds on Ida's mount;
   She could forgive each wrong the mocking gay,
   And loving them a purer soul to Heaven convey.

Then ye, who never tasted aught but joy,
   Reach out your arms and guide your sister home ;
Upbraid her not ; too much, alas ! is her alloy,
   From port to port, in this domain to roam ;
A guilty wretch to pray—to weep—to foam.
   Why chide her then, when conscience's double darted sting,
Confusion scattered into Reason's dome ?
   O, let her ear with consolation ring,
   Until her soul, once freed, its self does upward wing.

O, Leon! Leon dear! where art thou now ?
   Dost ever think of thy poor Madelaine ?
Say, "yes,"—say, "yes," and I to heaven will vow
   No more to weep, and be content again.
Then let the world look on me with disdain,
   And hatred to the offspring of its lore ;
I that disdain defy, and hatred's reign,
   If loved I were, as when, in days of yore,
   On pinions swift, our merry songs would homeward soar.

O Leon, dear! I suffered much indeed,
   Since thou hast gone, and left me quite alone ;
An unprotected mother's heart will bleed
   With direful woes to her, as yet, unknown,
To see her child in bitter anguish groan.
   Then come, my Leon! come! and claim thy son ;
For our past wrongs the future shall atone ; —
   O Gods ! there's naught on earth that I would shun,
   To make this home, a sacred shrine beneath the sun.

O Venus! Goddess of resistless love !
   A charm I crave which may a lustre shed,
(But equalled in the firmament above,

Where angels smile upon their starry bed,)
O'er my frail form—thy magic beauty—net.
And thou, O Juno! as I'll make amends,
Chaste Iris, let her dazzling rainbow spread,
   'Neath Jove's celestial throne! Leon repents,
   By Pallas guided, homeward now he wends.

O, martial queen! from thy celestial seat,
   Let fervent prayers move thee to depart;
In mortal guise my life's destroyer meet,
   To plead my cause; until it touched his heart;
Unconquered maid, use thou resistless art.
   Reprove him kindly for deserting me,
Till guilty conscience makes his body smart;
   Then, with ambrosia, heal it by degree,
   And, with that pain, O! let his evil habit flee.

And thou, O Cupid! flame him with desire,
   And finish what Minerva has begun;
And kindle in his bosom Love's own fire,
   Which, from his heart, through throbbing veins will run,
As in that hour when me he wooed and won,
   With burning words;—then to my fond embrace,
Thou blue-eyd maid! repentant, speed him on.
   Ecstatic, meet I'll his impassioned gaze,
   Which, 'gainst my will has set my soul ablaze.

In vain this outburst of a frantic joy.—
   In vain invoke the spirits from above;
A man who aimed at naught, save to destroy
   A guileless maiden, could not truly love;
His hungry passion stilled—then had enough.
   Though vows in torrents poured from heaving chest,
And studied gestures hid the villain rough,
   While fouler purpose nourished in his breast,
   A fiendish deed, which men abhor and Gods detest.

But to destroy me!—Madelaine, the coy!
   Me! the lovely, virtuous village-girl!

For *that* didst thou those subtle ways employ?
 For *that alone* didst steal this treasured pearl,
Which, since enjoyed by thee, will—does—must hurl
 Me, young and headlong, into Pluto's arms?
Hell's massive iron gates, let him unfurl,
 That it may yet receive the faded charms—
The envied prize, which reptiles draws, without alarms.

Thou, cursed, inhuman fiend! tell, why didst lure
 A maiden, from her childhood's happy home?
Inflict a wound, which age could not endure,
 To swiftly send fond parents hence to roam
No more on earth but rest within her womb?
 Efface the smile which, on a mother's brow,
Serenely hung, but flung, as from the tomb,
 A weeping pain o'er her bland cheek! oh! how
Can I but loathe thee and dire vengeance vow?

Oh! may black Hecate, with grim Ate leagued,
 Their ruthless legions joined, against thee send;
To chase thee forth through deserts—mountains peaked,
 With flickering hope thy weak'ning senses blend,
Until, at last, thy very heartstrings rend
 With deep remorse; onward, onward stride,
A solitary man, whose sufferings end
 Not in the grave, but then, with demons ride,
On nipping air, to moan through black and dismal night.

But, ere thy soul from mouldering body flees,
 And life's brief candle spends its flickering light:
May plague and torment never with thee cease
 To keenly pain; but ever on in spite
Of far-fetched groans, live in perpetual fright.
 May Friendship, Love or mildly soothing Hope,
Ne'er more in concord in thy heart abide.
 But desolate their shrine—with Discord cope,
And thus, with plague and strife thy miseries but ope.

No, no! I'm mad! I will not curse thee so;
   And never more with disappointment rail;
Let with the past be buried every woe,
   Forgetting all that could to memory hail
What years have traced—the causes of my wail.
   Though not thy spouse—my darling's father still
Thou art; therefore, a gentle, stirring gale
   May sweep thee on time's everflowing rill,
   Unscathed by grief or any other earthly ill.

Then when, perchance, thou meetst a storm-toss'd sail,
   On which, embarked, a lonely wanderer skims
The waters floating to that sylvan vale,
   Where sorrow not our weary twinklings dims.
Then, think of me, who, thus forsaken, stems
   The dashing waves and ceaseless blasts of Time.
'Twere but a tho't—and yet 'twould please my whims;
   And I will bless thee, though it were a crime,
   And thus, a blessing thee—forgiving, leave this clime.
Louisville, Ky., February, 1858.

Lines from an Album.

This spotless sheet, so pure and fair,
   As virgins in their bowers,
Henceforth shall be my harbinger
   Of love and friendship—kindred flowers.

Receive it back;—O, chide it not,
   For having lost its purity;
Thy name it lisped and nobly thought,
   Thereby regaining chastity.

Accept it then, and, with it, that
   Which, henceforth, must be one;
Its will and mine these lines begot,
   They crave a heart to rest upon.

14*

So share with them thy love-o'erflowing heart,
  Which will be kind when all beside is cold ;
They greet thee with an humble youth's regard,
  Who'd utter more, but dares not be so bold.

Regard! O, what am I to hide that passion,
  Which burns within with an everlasting flame ;
Regard ! a word alone for men of fashion,
  Whom love divine not as adherents claim.

O, let me breathe, fair one, that holy name,
  At whose sweet shrine ev'n angels knelt ;
Sensations, which, on high, their birthright claim,
  And are by mankind here so strongly felt.

So forget not fond girl, when memory brings near,
The friends that've loved, and those that were dear,
To grant me one tear, and happy I'll be,
To know that my ADA has shed it for me ;
Though parted from thee, by unavoidable fate,
To wander abroad in sun and in shade,
O'er deserts much shunned, by men of this clime,
Yet, with pleasure I'll kneel this prayer to chime :
"May our Heavenly Father show thee nothing but bliss,
The love of yon world, with the tenderness of this.   [brave,
May He surround thee with friends, who are constant and
First, shield thee on earth ; last, mourn thee in the grave.
May He keep thee in health, and crown thy fair head,
With silvery locks, when youth's pleasures have sped,
And bless thee as parent, though I will have gone,
To dwell with my Maker, beyond the proud sun.
O, know then that Rolla, on high will love thee the same,
As when in his May-days to woo thee he came.

LOUISVILLE, Ky., April, 1858.

The Dying Maid.

Oh, mother, dear! why weepest thou,
  And why escaped these mournful sighs?
Why now, so sorrowful thy brow,
  And restless thy pearl-gushing eyes?

I need not ask, who feels as though
  Sad days were drawing to a close;
Too few have been the joys below—
  It pleases *Him* to end my woes.

So weep not, mother, when I part,
  And nestle around *His* heavenly throne;
An angel, mother, thee to guard
  Will I be then, when thence I'm gone.

Oh, mother, dear! come near me now!
  I wish to see thee smile once more—
His will be done, then let's submissive bow,
  He'd plant me on the upper-shore.

So calm thyself, my mother, dear!
  Though this faint breathing be a sign,
That Death's cold fingers harbor near,
  To whom my soul this body must resign.

Stay mother dear, for I am dying—
  Let me not die in stranger's hands;
So mother, mother! cease this sighing,
  And note thy daughter's last demands.

Or wilt thou leave me, ere mine eye
  Has said farewell to joyous sight?—
On thee, I fain would look my last good-bye,
  So, mother, stay—all else seems night.

Louisville, March, 1858.

Hymn.

Let us send our voice imploring,
   To Jehovah's starry seat;
To our God this song be soaring,
   Which will mercy for us plead,
     On this happy, happy day,
     For Jehovah hears us pray.

Here united are we meeting,
   In thy house this Sabbath day;
Let Thy presence give us greeting,
   As we chant this simple lay,
     O, descend to dwell among
     Thine own people's joyous throng.

We now consecrate this temple
   To high Heaven's noble Lord;
Full with joy, we now assemble,
   And to pious themes resort.
     O, forgive the sins of all
     Who have sought this sacred wall.

Give us Light, whilst we are steering
   In this dark, too dark a path;
Dwell among us and be cheering
   The poor victims of thy wrath;
     We'll obey Thy dread commands,
     Though we live in foreign lands.

For Messiah are we waiting,
   Who will take us to our home;
May our glory not be fading,
   From great Judah's sons that roam,
     In all lands to chant a lay,
     On this joyous Sabbath day.

Louisville, July, 1858.

THIS POEM

IS RESPECTFULLY INSCRIBED

To Mrs. MAGGA KILMER, Poetess,

OF STURGIS, MICHIGAN.

Jonathan and David.

It must be he;—I hear his voice—'tis he;—
  These words so few, oh! mournfully they sound:
" Is not the arrow far escaping thee?"
  The echo does my sealed doom resound.
Already see I him his warsteed mount,
  And cry aloud, "'gainst David will I go."—
Alas; for aye inspiring trumpets sound
  War's thundering peal, where Jordan's waters flow,
  Till Saul has humbled and laid David low.

I know my fate, yet murmur will I not,
  But bear it as the Lord's Anointed should;
And fly from him, who, like some angry God,
  Through green-eyed jealousy destroys the good,
And braves the meek of his selected suit.
  This arrow whist sings dangers to mine ear,
Pronouncing haughty Saul less bold than lewd,
  Who, actuated by pale-painted Fear,
  Now seeks the life, he once endangered with his spear.

O, Jonathan, my friend! may God reward
  Thee! noble son of this wrath-kindled chief—
Thou need'st not speak, more woe thy looks report,
  Than clattering thunder could from heaven heave,
To silence Hope, and this fond heart to cleave.
  I know, full well, that I must leave this sphere,
And that our interview can be but brief:
  Yet, stay awhile, for I must shed a tear,
  Or else the heart will break, which faintly beateth here.

The royal prince glares on some silvery star!
 The youthful swain thinks o'er his destined doom;
The queen of night now mounts her jeweled car,
 Her silent journey calmly to resume,
Serenely smiling at earth's pale-faced gloom,
 The vampire does his lonely flight renew—
The shard-borne beetle, from the haunted tomb,
 Sends now his drowsy hum o'er waters blue,
 Where silver-footed Thetis wooes the sword-winged mew

Now calmly musing in deep revery,
 O'er what hath chanced on this now slumbering day,
Their thoughts float down the stream of memory,
 In search of flowers which ne'er will decay,
But bloom on earth, then find to heaven their way.
 They found but one—'t was ivy-mantled Hope;
Branched out on leaf-crowned Faith's sky-mounting spray.
 Which grows in hearts whose portals only ope
 To let our conscience with our passions cope.

O, noble youth! why gaze at placid skies,
 And watch each cloudlet in his cloistered march;
Why note the snow-fleeced dove which restless flies
 In search of her stray mate on air-tossed barge,
To carry plaints around the star-paved arch.
 Why contemplate o'er what has been decreed
By Him whose fires the sandy deserts parch;—
 Look up, fond swain, God's own advances meet,
 Whose humble agent does for thine own safety plead.

Though Duty and mild Friendship plead their case,
 Who nobly do defend their warm debates;
And Duty calls that son a recreant base,
 Who, with his sire's avowed opponents mates:
Yet Friendship's train re-enters Reason's gates,
 To urge the claim her conscience does attest,
When, from her brow the slumbering pallor fades,

As she exclaims: son! love thy parents best,
Yet more, thy God, who says, *to friend and foe be just.*

Then thou, fair swain, O listen to my tale—
    Thy life, our royal host will never spare :
For, ere the cunning fox does leave his trail,
    And stiff-backed wolf stalks back into his lair—
Ere nightingales with music fill the air,
    To bid the Day-God's fiery charioteer,
His foaming steeds, to brave the east, prepare,
    King Saul, in corselet mailed, and armed with spear,
    Will sally through yon creaking gates to meet thee here.

Then fly, my David, fly, and shun the foe,
    Who fain would take thy life, but gave me mine;
It was *the friend*, that stayed the pending blow,
    It is *the son*, who would his life resign,
Could he the father's save, through his decline;—
    If fortune smiles on thee, oh, spare him, swain;
In unsought mercy, let thy glory shine,
    And to my royal sire show no disdain,
    Nor with *thy* javelin seal the pages of his reign.

Hold, hold, great heir! and torture me no more,
    With words which, like some dagger, pierce my heart;
But me command and, from my heart's deep core,
    Shall homage ooze, and meek obedience dart.
Then prince, have for my feelings some regard,
    And learn that David ne'er would harm a hair
Of those whom thou art pleased to guard.
    Then rest in peace, and further pleading spare,
    Whom Jonathan does love, to save shall be my care.

Then cease the language which does wound me so,
    And breathe this message into Michæl's ear :
When flying faster than the fork-horned roe,
    O'er craggy peaks where wolves and tigers steer—
When Saul has wed her to some favorite peer,

And took from me, my dearest—dearest wife—
O, tell her, then, to shed a single tear,
    For him who wanders through this lonely life,
    A living corpse who sups, alas, on woes and strife.

And thou great prince, some rustic swain engage,
    To drive my flock around the ridgy steep;
Who'll teach the browsing lamb, of tender age,
    To climb the peak and over rocks to leap;
And who at nights will, to my goats and sheep,
    Pipe drearily some simple lay of mine,
While God will, over them, his vigil keep,
    To make them happy, when alone I'll pine,
    In lands where dwelt the giant Philistine.

              But see!
The East is bathing in a golden flame,
    And warbling lark greets now the new-born day;
Yet, I am here, yon monarch's hunted game,
    Once more to look on thee, and then go pray;—
Oh, whither, whither, shall I wind my way?
    In what lone desert will I safety find?
O God! he comes! he comes, in war's array!
    King Saul, who, with his steel-clad warriors, joined;
    Adieu; adieu; keep ever David in thy mind.
LOUISVILLE, July, 1858.

The Burial of De Soto.

'Twas the silent twilight hour of a new born eve.
Beyond the gold-capped hills of the blushing west,
In rosy brilliancy, majestically cloistered, descended,
His flashy beams, athwart darting, the sun.
His last glimm'ring rays were still kissing
The towering tops of each stately oak,
When, pale as the virgin's corpse in her snowy shroud,
From a *seeming* chaos in the far-off east emerged,

With her starry train in grave attendance,
Th' ethereal vault ascending, the silver moon.

For a short, short while, all nature seemed to slumber—
Not a leaf stirred to break the spell of gently onward stealing
    night.
Slowly the solemn queen her jewel-studded chariot drove,
Near the Seraph-guarded throne of propitious Jove,
Faintly gazing on the sleeping world beneath,
Freezing the placid cloudlets with the ghastly glare.

Now, melancholy pale sat brooding in the lap of darkness,
And night, her sable curtains gently threw around
The dying eve's roseate hue—but list;
A soft wind is breathing, and each mossy leaf,
Which, trembling, hung upon some tender twig,
Now sends a wailing forth, on nature's humming voice,
E'en the calmly flowing waters, addressing the moon,
In plaintive discourse, to moan began loudly:
As on the silver-sheeted Mississippi lonely lounged,
A single sail, on which a solemn duty was performed.
Upon the deck, a band of heroes grieving stood,
To lay De Soto—Hernando de Soto—in his watery grave.
Aye, *they* wept, who often nature, with contempt, defied,
And bade the starting tear drop back into the briny orb,
To hide the heart's deep grief with a stoic's pride.

Yes, *they* wept—wept bitter, burning tears, who,
After having left what's prized, upon the Spanish coast,
Hence followed their commander, now no more,
Where Cortez and Pizarro gained great wealth and fame,
Who, intoxicated with success, have roused De Soto's pride;
Aye, he swore, on ambition's shrine, to outrival them in fame,
Or else ignobly perish on the hunting ground.

    *   *   *   *   *   *   *   *   *   *

In vain, for wealth he searched, yet more his glory
*First** to behold "*the father of the Floating Waters.*"
Long after Pamphile's gold again has turned to dust,
And Cortez and Pizarro's fame is dimmed by brighter stars—
Then yet De Soto lives in every navigator's heart,
Whose bark floats down Mississippi's noble stream ;
Whilst wailing zephyrs steal o'er its foaming billows,
To chant a solemn, solemn dirge at midnight hours,
For him who, *wondering*, gazed upon those dancing waves,
Then thought naught else so grand a monument,
As the proud waters, which, o'er his lonely grave,
Keep up a melancholy cadence, till Time's no more.   .

LOUISVILLE, August, 1858.

---

*In April, 1541, De Soto discovered the Mississippi, being
the first European, who visited that River.

Lines to my Sister.

O, dear Sister in the Dream-land,·
 Where sweet angels have their homes,
Whisper love from Upper Eden,
 To thy Willie, who now roams
On this earth, to joy a stranger,
 And to happiness unknown—
A deserted, lonely being,
 Like a bark on billows thrown.

Dost remember, how in childhood,
 We each other would caress,
As we gamboled in the valley,
 And each grove gave soft recess?
Dost remember how our mother,
 In simplicity, would gaze,
With a pride but known to parents,
 On her children's smiling face !

Ah me, gone to thee, sweet Ada,
    Is our mother, there to rest,
Where her good and noble actions,
    In bold letters, stand expressed.
And our father's wearied spirit,
    Has already followed where
He forever may keep vigil
    O'er his orphan in despair.

Once so happy was thy brother,
    In his manhood's younger days,
Ere grim death had taken from him,
    What the heart yearns to embrace,
With a love so pure and holy,
    And a trembling tenderness,
That the loss thereof is bitter,
    Far too bitter to express.

Yet there's comfort, blue-eyed sister,
    In the thought of leaving woe,
Ere the earth again be shrouded
    In a robe of fleecy snow.
And 'tis sweet to *feel* approaching,
    With a step so light and sure,
Yon proud monarch, with a pass-word,
    To the chamber of the pure.

For they call me cold and cruel,
    And pronounce me void of love —
I do seem a spectre gloomy,
    And am smiling not enough.
O, my sister, is thy Willie,
    By his comrades *rightly* known?
Do they judge by his appearance,
    And forget *that he's alone?*

In my bosom's sacred temple,
    Where no earthly passions reign,

All alone, unnoticed, weepeth,
    Love neglected — but in vain.
Oh, Just Father! show me mercy,
    For the sin I now commit,
To be wishing myself buried,
    As for earth I am unfit.
LOUISVILLE, Ky., Dec., 1858.

Lines to Nathan Mayer.

No longer shall my fingers sweep the heavenly lyre,
Whose gentle strains betrayed the secrets of my soul;
Since only grief and sorrow now my themes inspire,
To chant the feelings that my weakness can't control.

The harp, my friend, has ceased to mourn my bitter fate,
For now it shattered lies upon the cold — cold ground;
Its parting song still greets me from yon starry gate,
With cadence, Peris breathed 'round Eden's sparkling fount.

'Twas I who broke the chords, that wept when I did weep,
And soothed to sleep th' afflictions of the heart's deep core;
Therefore the fragments all shall with me in the deep,
In concert rest, when soul and song sought heaven's shore.

But oh, my friend! beseech me not to chime of bliss,
Nor tune my heart to warble forth a joyous lay;
For brothers' — sisters' kind applause on earth I miss, —
Then cease imploring — madness only makes me gay.

In bacchanalian feasts the mind forgets its grief,
And late carousings oft dispel the hovering gloom;
Their charms but weave a brittle band around the sheaf,
Where pleasures wild consign affections to the tomb.

'Tis true, kind friends may greet me with as bland a smile
As ever graced a brother or a sister's brow; —

But where the chiding tenderness devoid of guile,
To censure wrongs and show the justice they avow ?

The slanderer too oft distils into the mind
Some poisonous tale to steal perhaps an only friend ;—
He speaks of naught save where he can some errors find,
For Envy hides the little good he should defend.

And then the fondness—oh! the trifles that can melt
The yearning heart to ecstacy and ceaseless joy,
From brothers'—sisters' lips can never be repelled,
Since malice dares not there vile stratagems employ.

But then, dear friend, thy song bedecked mine eyes with tears,
An emblem of the gratitude I can't express;
As morning dew to strength cerulean rears,
So thine appeal revived in me the spark of tenderness.

Therefore I pledge thee love and friendship ever more,
To purely last beyond this narrow span of life,
Until kind fate my spirit does to Him restore,
That praying for thee will in happiness be rife.

Yet, here on earth, may health and pleasure be thy lot,
Where cherished kin will greet thee with an honest mien ;
Whilst I resign my weary spirit unto God,
Since I am but the wreck of what I once have been.

LOUISVILLE, Ky., Jan., 1859.

Nature's Gentleman.

WE but deceive ourselves, to call those just,
Who are so in their petty dealings with mankind;
For 'tis not he, who, *out of fear*, commits no wrong,
Evading crime, that's nature's gentleman ;
While his faint heart and soul for aye does yearn for that
Which *cowardice*, but not his *conscience*, keeps away from reach.
Nor he the one who should be called the truly just,

15*

Who scatters alms, *that he be thought* a generous man:
Whilst evermore his tongue gives loose to slanders vile,
To injure those whose arm's too weak to make a mighty fist.
Nor is it he who would offend no living man,
And yet *unmoved*, sees him abused by ev'ry knave.;
That man in whose lone house dwells poverty,
Which drove away the thousands of those seeming friends
That, in prosperity would gather 'round his hearth.
Nor he, my friends, who gives his praise to him alone,
Who *safely* rests in fame's anointed dome,
But finds no cheering words to stir the mounting soul,
Which struggles hard with fate, but's doomed to struggle on
    in vain.

'Tis he alone, that's worthy of our praise,
Who boldly dares to check the proud and overbearing mind
Resenting not, when he may, *safely*, vengeance take,
For wrongs inflicted on him by his fellow men.
He is the just, whose conscience even spurns the secret tho't,
Which would disgrace his manhood in his Maker's sight,
Whose image he does wear, within the chambers of his soul
Which with just deeds does mark his manly brow,
Pronouncing him at once, a Man—Creation's Monarch!
   LOUISVILLE, January, 1859.

The Ivy and the Oak: Their Origin.

'Tis moonlight 'round the gates of Paradise
And silver beams sleep on the cedar's boughs,
In beauty vying with the ray that flies
From mid day's sun to tinge the angels' brows,
Who, on yon flaming portals keep their guard,
Their blazing weapons piercing realms of space,
Like meteors who from their own eyes depart,
With bright effulgence mankind to amaze.

Balmed zephyrs too steal from closed Eden's wall,
To greet with sighs the scarcely peopled earth,
Deploring Eve's and Adam's mighty fall —
How Abel died, when he to death gave birth.

With curses loaded, Cain, the parricide
Awaits the setting of the burning sun,
In shades of darkness to commence his flight,
Since he the day now fears to look upon.

At last he turns to meet his sister's gaze,
And say, "Farewell," ere he now goes abroad;
For all retraced their steps — yet Adah stays,
With Enoch on her arms; her only thought
To follow him, where'er his lot be found,
In zones where snows ne'er melt, or sunbeams parch
The weary foot on deserts' sandy ground,
Where reptiles creep and fierce hyenas march.

"O, Adah!" thus commenced the banished Cain,
"Why follow'st not thy sire and mother Eve?
Why not lament with them thy brother slain?
Why does thy bosom not with sorrow heave?

Behold! in yon sweet grove where lilies bloom,
Thy parents now inter dead Abel's corse;
Look! how the skies a deeper hue assume,
And stars wax dim as midnight winds grow hoarse.

So leave me, sister, for I must be gone,
And seek the shelter Eve denies me here;
Forget me not, my Adah! thou alone
Wilt pity whom mankind have cause to fear.

Jehovah's wrath rests on the parricide,
And sire and Eve abhor me for the deed,
Which sends me forth a criminal to-night,
To brave the danger by thy God decreed.

So stay behind, and teach my son to love
His hapless father in thy fond caress;
Be thou to Enoch gentler than a dove,
While I deserted walk the wilderness,
A victim singled out for punishment.

Jehovah stamped this crime upon my head,
That all mankind may cease to be my friend,
And slay me for the blood these hands have shed.
O! curse me never"———

               " Curse thee, Cain? no! no!"
Exclaimed Eve's daughter, trembling at his side;
" I can but grieve—my nature wills it so;
Where love once dwelled, hate never can abide.

Behold! thy Enoch stretches out his hands,
His father to caress in childish glee;
Take hold of them, for we to other lands
Will now go forth, this grove no more to see."

Once more they gazed around the slumbering scene
Inhaling the perfume of drooping violets,
Ere they departed from the dewy green,
Where cedars shadow Eden's fragrant beds.

Two Seraphs winged their flight from sky to earth
And lit on Cain and Adah's swimming eyes;
Saw his remorse—sweet Adah's gentle worth,
In his entreaties and her mild replies.

From out their orbs each stole one glittering tear,
And buried them beneath dead Abel's grave,
From which High Heaven was pleased the Oak to rear,
With Ivy 'round his trunk, love's monument to save.

LOUISVILLE, Ky., May 25, 1859.

To Susan.

Whilst fondly I gaze, o'er the distant far;
Where naught can be seen, save some illumining star;
Remembrance of thee does paint into view,
With colors so vivid—the form of my " Sue."

Though in darkness enshrouded, all around me does seem,
And no voices are heard save the owl's wily scream;
To think thee so near me, night changes her hue,
And owl's boding grows fainter, when nearer to " Sue."

In slumber, now basketh the lowly and proud,
Unconscious of evil, that's lurking about;
But, terrorless to me, are Ate's whole crew;
I fear not their vengeance, so they spare my dear " Sue."

Though rich men are boasting of ill-gotten wealth,
I crave not their gold—I but pray for good health;
With gold dust a plenty, you'll find but a few,
Whose hearts are as constant as mine to my " Sue."

And if costly their cloak, and more winning, their smile
That is hiding a heart, full of baseness and guile;
And be seeming more lovely, may yet be less true,
Than poor Will., in jeans garments, has been to his " Sue."

So, sleep softly, sweet maiden, and know thyself blessed,
In having, of lovers, the truest—the best;
Whilst remembrance, to-night, does paint into view,
With colors so vivid—the form of my "Sue."

LOUISVILLE, KY.

Farewell to Louisville.

The sun is sinking in the west:
　　Athwart his rays now fly;
Yet on yon elms they manifest
　　Their splendor ere they die.
A girdle of a golden hue
Encircles the Ethereal blue,
　　To bid the laughing day farewell.
But where, O, where, can I perceive
A single heart that's touched by grief,
　　In list'ning to my parting knell.

E'en earth enshrouded in a gown
　　Of sable colors mourns
The sun that parched what man has sown,
　　From eastern to the western bourns.
His beams revive the drooping flowers,
When raindrops fall in gentle showers,
　　Upon the verdure-skirted field.
His good,—men cherish in the soul,
And pardon, what he can't control,—
　　Stern Nature's laws wont be repealed.

'Tis true, I'm frail—but who is not,
　　Of mortals, apt to sin?
Then have more mercy for our God,
　　His image left within.
There is no villain quite so base,
But has a conscience to erase,
　　What evil passions may dictate;
Redeeming traits, like stars at night,
When darkness makes them shine more bright,
　　Exceed th' extent of what ye hate.

My faults are few: a thousand worse,
　　In scorpion minds conceived,

Base churls retailed to be my curse,
    And baser ones believed.
Let such these wrongs exaggerate,
Which curs for my destruction made,
    Through fear I might in spite ascend
Fame's steeple, as I onward march,
O'er thorny paths to Glory's arch,
    Where upstarts vain will fail to blend.

To foe and friend I bid adieu,   ,
    For I will leave this spot,
Where moaning winds around me blow
    The anger of my God.
Where malice wounded honest pride
And stole the lamp whose silvery light,
    Alone I courted on my path ;
For which my heart is bleeding still,
And tears escape this tender rill,
    That never sparkled inborn wrath.

O! let me now enjoy sweet peace,
    Afar from home and friend,
And prayers on each passing breeze,
    To God for you I'll send.
My days are short—my hours are few :
Be ye then kind who ne'er were true—
    With my poor soul 'twill soon be well ;
Then friends and foes! remembered still,
A sorry joy, against my will :
    Once more to you a fond Farewell.
SAVANNAH, Tenn., Sep., 1859.

In looking over the foregoing book, we discover several errors which escaped the attention of the proof reader. Most of them will be readily corrected by the intelligent reader. On page 97, the 10th line should read:
MORTARA.—Thou shalt not murder, vengeance is mine own;

www.ingramcontent.com/pod-product-compliance
Lightning Source LLC
Chambersburg PA
CBHW031117020726

47495CB00007B/2236